THE ROAD TO COSMOS

OTHER BOOKS BY BILL MEISSNER

Learning to Breathe Underwater [poetry]

The Sleepwalker's Son [poetry]

Twin Sons of Different Mirrors [poetry]

American Compass [poetry]

Hitting into the Wind [short stories]

THE ROAD TO

COSMOS

The Faces of an American Town

BILL MEISSNER

University of Notre Dame Press

Notre Dame, Indiana

Manufactured in the United States of America

The author and publisher gratefully acknowledge permission for the quotation
of lines from "Darkness on the Edge of Town" by Bruce Springsteen.
Copyright © 1978 Bruce Springsteen (ASCAP). Reprinted by permission.
International copyright secured. All rights reserved.

Library of Congress Cataloging-in-Publication Data

Meissner, William, 1948–
The road to Cosmos : the faces of an American town / Bill Meissner.
p.   cm.
ISBN-13: 978-0-268-03501-3 (pbk. : alk. paper)
ISBN-10: 0-268-03501-6 (pbk. : alk. paper)
1. Middle West—Social life and customs—Fiction.   2. Eccentrics and
eccentricities—Fiction.   I. Title.

PS3563.E38R63   2006
813'.54—dc22

2006024964

∞ *The paper in this book meets the guidelines for permanence and durability of*
the Committee on Production Guidelines for Book Longevity of the Council on
Library Resources.

For my wife Chris and son Nate,
always the greatest companions on the road

Also for my mother, Julia Meissner, the original storyteller,
for her endless support and encouragement,
and in memory of my father, Leonard Meissner

CONTENTS

ACKNOWLEDGMENTS

Thanks to Chris for her loving, insightful advice during the writing and revising of these stories.

I would also like to thank Jack Driscoll, and those members of the St. Cloud State University creative writing staff who have supported my writing over the years.

I thank the following organizations for awards that supported the writing of these stories:
- Loft-McKnight Foundation for a Loft McKnight Award of Distinction for Fiction
- National Endowment for the Arts for a Creative Writing Fellowship
- Minnesota State Arts Board for an Individual Artist's Grant
- Loft-McKnight Foundation for a Loft-McKnight Fellowship
- St. Cloud State University Alumni Fund for Fiction Grants

The following stories were awarded PEN/NEA Syndicated Fiction Awards: "The Last of the Rain" (selected by Kurt Vonnegut, Jr.), "The Waking of the Carrots," and "The Hunting Jacket." The stories were syndicated and published nationally in a number of Sunday picture magazines, including *The Miami Herald, The Oregonian,* and *The Minneapolis Star Tribune.* "The Last of the Rain" was reprinted in *Umass Magazine.*

The following stories were syndicated by the Fiction Network of San Francisco: "A Road So Smooth, and So Close to Home" and "The Handkerchief." "A Road So Smooth" was reprinted in *Lake Country Journal.*

The stories in this collection appeared in the following publications:

Minneapolis/St. Paul Magazine:
   "Train Whistles, Flights of Geese," "Seven Stories about the Old American Cars"
Minneapolis Tribune Sunday Picture Magazine:
   "The Last of the Rain," "The Handkerchief," "A Road So Smooth, and So Close to Home"
Fiction Network Magazine:
   "A Road So Smooth, and So Close to Home"
The Northern Review:
   "The Rescue"
Minnesota Monthly:
   "Fainting," "Fake Fights," "The Things You Lose"
Missouri Review:
   "Freddie and the Dreamers"
Witness (Sports in America Anthology):
   "The Hunting Jacket"
26 Minnesota Writers (anthology):
   "The Tug of War," "One Egg at a Time"
Believers (forthcoming anthology):
   "The Woman Who Dreamed Elvis"
North American Review:
   "The Car Circle"

"The Rescue" was nominated for a Pushcart Prize.

x

THE ROAD TO COSMOS

"Sometimes it had seemed to me when, as a young man, I sat at the window of that room, that each person who passed along the street below, under the light, shouted his secret up to me. . . . I had thought then, on such evenings, that I could tell all of the stories of all the people of America."

—Sherwood Anderson, comments on the writing of
Winesburg, Ohio in "The Finding"

"Lives on the line where dreams are found and lost,
I'll be there on time and I'll pay the cost,
For wanting things that can only be found
In the darkness on the edge of town."

—Bruce Springsteen, "Darkness on the Edge of Town"

PART ONE

SMALL DANCES
TO AN UNHEARD SONG

SKIP REMEMBERS
The Tug of War

■ ■ My father was a lawn mower. His scent was not fresh, but pungent, like cut weeds, and his lines were even, the grass always mowed in columns so straight you could measure the horizon by them. You could keep time by him, too—his steady gait as he walked up the stairway, the few floorboards he hadn't fixed creaking under his weight. You could keep time by him, drumming his fingers slowly on the molding as he stood in the doorway, looking not at me but beyond me, into a corner of my bedroom, then announcing that we were going to mow the lawn.

I never understood the logic of lawn mowing when I was seventeen; I just knew that it always came at the wrong time. He had the uncanny knack—or maybe it was a conscious plan—to begin the lawn mowing routine on Friday nights after dinner, when I was just about to go out. I knew an old Rambler waited outside for me to drive it. My buddies from high school scanned the street for me as they leaned against the pillars of their porches, carving their initials in the wood. And there were girls, their long legs stepping out of the north shore of the lake, girls toweling their bare shoulders in the dusk as they stood at the edge of the beach. These thoughts were calling me, and I found myself leaning toward them in my pale blue button-down shirt, and always, at that moment, my father was standing there: a thick brick wall suddenly blocking my open window.

His voice grated against my ears: "I want to get it done before the weekend."

My shrug must have bothered him as I stared at the striped pattern on my bedspread. I suppose there was a look of irritation on my face, too, but because he wasn't staring right at me, but at the tiny, spreading cracks in the plaster in the corner of my room, he probably didn't see it.

I usually countered his lawn mowing orders with something like "I was just going out."

"Well, you're not," he'd retort, his words chiseled, stony.

As he stood there, I pictured that old mower: its chipped tan enamel paint, its underside a dark green, plastered with wet grass. At times, its hollow aluminum bar seemed to pull at me as I paced the half acre behind our house. Other times, when I was nearly finished, I pushed at it to go faster, but the mower seemed to suddenly gain weight and slow me down.

4

*　*　*

That Friday evening, the impasse reached, we each stood in our silence a moment: my silence was thick and dark, like a pool of oil. His silence was like a net: all the knots too tight and wanting to loosen a little, but afraid to. He turned his stocky body and walked slowly down the stairway, knowing full well that I'd follow him. I might take my dress shirt off, wad it up into a ball and slam it to the floor, but I'd follow him.

As I walked behind him in his undershirt and work pants, I began to see my life in the future. I thought about how every step I took on that creaking stairway was like another genuflection, another nod of agreement to his plan, another cower to his rule. I saw a quick vision of myself someday, in an undershirt and work pants, walking down some creaking stairway toward a paint-chipped toolshed.

So when I got to the base of the stairs and watched his wide silhouette cross the window shades toward the shed in the backyard, I grabbed my keys from the end table, stepped out the door, turned the opposite direction, and ran toward my car.

The Rambler's door opened easily for me, its hinges oiled. It was my car, it always had been. My father had bought it for me at an Army surplus auction for my sixteenth birthday. I gave it a tune-up and repainted it, covering its Army green with a layer of metallic red so the car had some semblance of coolness for a high school junior. When I turned the key, the car started quickly. Backing out past his tan Chrysler parked on the grass, I saw him turn the corner with the lawn mower and just stop there. But he didn't look up—just kept his eyes fixed on the ground in front of him, as if he'd just come onto a patch of bristling weeds made of iron, weeds he knew his mower could never cut.

"Blade's too dull," I'd often complain to him after I mowed. It seemed to me that the weeds and long grass simply bent over beneath it, then sprang back up again in a few days. "Can't we get a new mower? Or at least get this thing sharpened?"

"That blade's fine, Skip," he'd always tell me. "You just have to slow down a little when you mow." Then he'd put one foot on the flat top of the Briggs and Stratton motor, a motor that never quit on him, he often told me, not once. A motor that started on the first pull in spring even after sitting in the shed for a long, cold winter.

*   *   *

That night I backed into the street and drove away without looking at him. *He can keep his damn mower*, I thought. *He can mow all night, for all I care. He can mow every lawn in Cosmos.* I drove for a half hour along the deserted county roads near the lake; the sun had set and the glow of my headlights seemed to be leading me where I needed to go. I rolled down the window, turned up the radio volume, and let rock 'n roll songs—like "Satisfaction" and "Mony Mony"—blare, distorted, through the speakers and into the country-side, each song an anthem for my freedom.

Then I saw a pair of lights flare up behind me. The car gained on me quickly, and I expected it to pass, but it didn't. As the car closed in, I recognized its silhouette. It was the Chrysler, and inside, that dark shape stiff behind the steering wheel, was my father. He stayed behind me, flashing his brights. I took my foot off the brake pedal and my Rambler coasted to the gravel shoulder. He eased the Chrysler close. I clicked the ignition off. For a few seconds, I felt short of breath, like I had just run a mile in gym class, and I could hear, through the dash, the hot engine of the Rambler ticking as it cooled. He stepped out of his car and walked slowly toward me, fol-lowing the white line at the edge of the asphalt road like a state trooper. He reached my rear fender. Without even thinking, I started the car and floored it. My old Rambler wasn't used to such accelera-tion, and the six cylinders stuttered beneath the hood a moment, but then it took off like I knew it could, spinning a cloud of gravel dust around my father.

I didn't know where I was going; I was just trying to lose my father, lose him, leave him far behind with his little world of orders and lawn mowers and perfectly straight columns.

In the rearview mirror, I saw his headlights closing the gap be-tween us. I knew the Chrysler had guts—that beast could do nearly 110 on an open stretch of asphalt. In seconds, his headlights edged within inches of my bumper, and I began to sweat as I glanced into the mirror, then back at my speedometer, which read 85, then into the mirror again. I was desperate, and I knew that after what I'd just done, there could be no slowing, no turning back. The Rambler didn't seem to have any power left; still, I kept pushing hard on the floored accelerator until it felt as though I might break through the floorboards and up to my knee.

It was then that I noticed another set of headlights behind the Chrysler, and, a few seconds later, a red cherry light stung my eyes.

I gasped and yanked my foot off the accelerator, as my father must have done at the same instant, because our cars, as if they were doing a dance, coasted gradually to a stop at the same time.

I stepped out of my car and walked on shaky legs back to my father, who stood on the shoulder next to the cop.

"What's goin' on here, Dwight?" Evan asked my father. Evan Schlueter was a county cop we'd known around Cosmos for years; my father was a member of the Knights of Columbus with him. Evan pointed the flashlight upward, and the shadows carved deep guilty creases in the skin of my father's face.

"Nothing," my father replied, his voice suddenly calm, controlled. "The boy here, well," he paused, faltering a moment, "the boy's having carburetor trouble with his car. I tried to fix it, told him to take it out for a run. Told him I'd follow him in case the car killed."

"You had to go *that* damn fast to test it?" Evan puffed. "Sure looked like some kind of race to me."

I could feel the arteries in my neck throbbing from the adrenaline. I knew that with a speeding ticket—at this speed, at least— I'd lose my license, which I'd had for only a year. My father knew that too.

"Well, you see, the car only killed at higher speeds," my father said, continuing his fabrication. "Runs like a top on city streets, though." He managed a chuckle.

Evan shook his head as he examined the laminated licenses we'd pulled from our wallets. He shined his flashlight at them, making them both appear thin, translucent. Typed in black, I saw my full legal name, the name my father gave me out of pride when I was born, the name I hated and never wanted to use: *Franklin Delano Roosevelt Carrigan.* "I don't know who the heck to ticket here," Evan said, "the lead car or the one who was following."

He paused a few seconds, rubbing his double chin as if to find a solution. "So I'm not going to ticket neither one of you." He pointed at my father. "Just take this as a warning, Dwight. You better take care of this boy, and clear up the problem on that Rambler some other way. You can't be out racing like a couple of teenagers."

*   *   *

After the squad car left, my father didn't say anything, just tipped his head back, looked at the opaque sky as if he was recognizing something, and then laughed a quick, sharp laugh. At that moment I felt maybe everything was okay. "Thanks, Dad," I said, trying to sound confident, though my nerves were tangled and sparking like crossed distributor wires. "I mean, for bailing me out."

He turned toward me and opened his big palm. "Give me the keys, Skip," he said, his voice flat, like a piece of tin.

"Huh?"

"Give me the damn keys. You're walking home." He took a step closer to me and spoke through gritted teeth. "You're walking until you're eighteen."

I lifted the keys, attached to a leather strap, from my pocket, lowered them into his palm, and he clenched them. But I didn't let them go; feeling a sudden rush of resistance, and thinking about the five long miles back to town, I held tight to my end of the leather strap.

In those few seconds, as we both pulled on the keys, I could feel the whole world pulling on us like a tug of war—the whole world pulling us together, pulling us apart at the same time.

Then the strangest thing happened. He released his grip and let them go, and the keys jingled against my knuckles. He closed his eyes. In the dim light, I tried to read his face, but I just couldn't figure it out. That was the thing about my father—I was always on the verge of understanding him, but I never quite could. He pivoted and marched toward the Chrysler. Opening the driver's side, he leaned on the wide tan door and looked at me a few seconds as if he were about to say something. Then he slipped behind the wheel.

For a moment an image of that tan lawn mower appeared in my head. I pictured it in a field: stained with oil, low on gas, sputtering, my father trying to cut a straight path through the long weeds and not really knowing how.

*   *   *

That night, the layer of clouds was thick, impenetrable, and no stars or moon appeared as we drove toward the horizon on that county road. When I glanced in the rearview mirror, the asphalt road was pitch black. I turned the radio down and stayed behind my father's car, our lights cutting a column through the darkness. At one point, his Chrysler seemed to hesitate a little, and I concentrated on keeping an even distance between our two cars. Not too far back, not too close. All the while, I couldn't help but focus on the taillights and wonder just how long I'd follow them and how far, their steady red eyes neither angry nor forgiving, but simply watching me all the way back to town.

The Tug of War

LILLY

The Demolition Derby Driver's Wife

■ ■ She sets up the tripod in the rickety grandstand, ready to begin

her filming, worries a little about what she might see through

the lens. Lilly makes sure everything's in focus, especially his

black Plymouth Fury with the number 777 painted on it in

crude white spray-paint—a car with the doors welded shut so

they'd never open again. It's a car Danny worked on with a

mechanic friend of his all last weekend, removing visors and

mirrors and door handles, wiring down the hood, pulling all

the glass out, reinforcing the frame with steel pipes so it could

absorb impact after brutal impact. With what seemed like so

much love, he stripped the car down to its bare essentials

while she sat in her shorts on an oil-stained parts box in the

back of the garage, drinking a Diet Coke and listening to the oldies channel on a plastic '50s radio. *A million starving kids in the world,* she thought as she watched, *and he's plugging a thousand dollars into this old car just so he can demolish it.*

Lately she really can't understand Danny's obsession, this demolition derby fever he's caught from somewhere. Though he's a manager at Excel Business Products in Cosmos, he's begun to watch derbies on TV on some obscure sports channel. He reads about them in *Circle Track Magazine,* and even worse, talks about them over dinner, saying things like "You floor it in reverse and then brace for the hit." These days, instead of invoices and sales, all he talks about is entering that Labor Day demo derby, the final derby of the year.

"But why?" she asked a few weeks ago at dinner.

"Because it might be fun," Danny replied. He tugged the neck of his gray T-shirt, a little too small for him lately.

"Fun? Strapped into a car that someone's bashing into? That's fun?"

"Well," he clarified, running his hand through his sandy hair so it rose a little in a James Dean pompadour, "maybe not fun then. But a challenge. Definitely a challenge."

"It's not challenge enough just to drive on the interstate?" She's referring to I-90, which passes on the edge of town, clogged with semis full of freight and livestock. There always seems to be a car flipped in the ditch when she takes that highway.

"No," he replied, a little friction sounding in his voice. "It's not."

With that, she stood from the table, picking up her water glass and clinking it loudly into the middle of her plate. He followed her to the dishwasher. "Come on," Danny said apologetically, but without any further explanation. He slid one arm around her waist. He never was much for words. "Come on, Lilly."

Her lips pursed in a tight line, she just kept rinsing her dishes, then sprayed the sink with a circular motion, the water making a hollow sound against the dulled aluminum.

* * *

She knows the dangers of demolition driving after watching a couple derbies at the Golden Spike Speedway on Sunday afternoons. And it's not just the whiplash and spinal injuries the drivers

11

have to guard against by using those neck and back braces. Once a car caught on fire, the hood bursting with flame as the panicked driver scrambled out of the window, jumped onto the track and ran to the safety of the grass infield; seconds later, the car erupted in a huge orange flower. She heard that a demo car's gas tank—sloshing with a couple gallons of yellow ultimate—is located next to the driver, and she wondered why.

"There's no other place to put it," Danny explained.

"But *right next* to the driver? It doesn't make sense."

"That's where they *always* put it," he sighed with finality, as if sitting that close to the potential fiery explosion was just something you did.

"Then you should wear a flame suit, at least."

"Aw," he flipped his hand in the air like he was swatting a gnat. Danny knew none of the drivers went all out like that, wearing one of those expensive flame-retardant white jumpsuits with Valvoline and Richard Petty and Goodyear patches plastered over them. If he wore one, instead of the standard jeans and a short-sleeved T-shirt, like the younger guys wore, it would appear that he was showing off, trying to be a kind of flashy I'm-Elvis-in-Vegas.

*   *   *

"Can I sit in it?" she asked when the car was finally done and the 777—his lucky number, he called it—was spray-painted on the door panel of the Fury.

"No."

"Come on. I want to drive it around the back lot a little," she said, just so she could get the feel of what he was up against.

"No," he repeated, this time a little more irritated.

"Why not?"

"You're just not driving it, that's all." His voice was a sharp piece of scrap metal. It was as if this vehicle, this repainted, stripped-down beast was his and his alone to tame. As if her job as a music teacher precluded her from even touching a machine like this.

As soon as he said that, she stomped out of the garage, bumping a box of spark plugs with her hip, the porcelain plugs clicking as they hit the concrete floor. She hated it when he talked like that to her; whenever he got dictatorial and arbitrary, her life felt like a one-way street she couldn't back out of. She knew Danny loved her, but it seemed like sometimes he had an ignition switch inside him that could easily be flipped. At those moments she didn't cross him; she just obeyed and shut up, on the outside at least. But on the inside, she seethed. On the inside, she pressed an accelerator to the floor.

*　　*　　*

But those discussions are several days back on the track; right now, she's setting up the camera for today's derby, like he asked her. He filmed a couple of the Sunday afternoon derbies last month, and the weird thing was that when he got the videotape home, he took it down to the den to edit it and set it to music. She pictured him setting it to heavy metal music, like Led Zeppelin or ACDC's "Back in Black," or maybe something moody like Bruce Springsteen's "Darkness on the Edge of Town," a song he played repeatedly on the cassette player of their car. But one Sunday evening, standing halfway down the stairway, she heard classical music wafting through the speakers. Vivaldi or Beethoven, she thought. She imagined each sudden impact syncopated exactly to Beethoven's Fifth Symphony: *Da da da dum. Da da da dum.* Or gliding through the mud until they stop suddenly, syncopated to a Schubert waltz: *Da-da-da-da-dah—thump thump, thump thump.*

*　　*　　*

13

As the cars roar up from the pits for the feature, she begins filming, focusing on the clay ramp where his number 777 noses up. The cars take their spots, seven cars on each side of the center track, all with their trunks facing their opponent's trunk, all with their engines revving so the cars shudder a little. Every car looks dented except for Danny's. The flagman in the black and white–striped shirt ceremoniously places a large watermelon in the center of the track, and the track announcer proclaims that the first driver to crush it gets an automatic fifty bucks. She watches her husband's dark-helmeted form through the lens and wonders what he could possibly be thinking or feeling right now. The announcer shouts, "Let's get ready to rumble!" and the crowd begins a dramatic countdown: five! four! three! . . .

The Demolition Derby Driver's Wife

It's like a countdown for a rocket launch, she thinks, and it seems like minutes pass between each number, the anxious blood rushing to her head, making her feel faint. But the two thousand fans— many of them overweight and munching corn dogs—think it's fun; they seem convinced that watching these big American cars collide until they're dented beyond recognition is a form of entertainment.

Two!…one! The exhaust pipes, spitting fire as they poke through the hood, roar so loud she has to plug her ears. The cars rush backward toward each other, and Danny's car squashes the watermelon with his big Firestone racing tire, causing the red pulp to splatter and the crowd to roar. Then the cars meet in the middle, crunching hard with the impact. She can feel the hit on Danny's car right in the center of her chest. They spin their wheels, pull themselves forward, then back in for another hit, then drag forward again. Danny told her he plans to aim for his opponent's back wheel, so he might break the axle and cripple the car. *A million disabled kids in the world,* she thought after he said that, *and my husband's goal is to cripple a 1978 Fairlane.* Even with the watered-down track and the mud, the vehicles still get up a good rate of speed, enough power to smack an opponent side-on and occasionally send the car airborne a few inches or even to flip it over. The goal out there is simple: to debilitate your opponent by popping his radiator with a white hissing cloud, by breaking his rear axle, or by jamming your bumper pipes into the steaming heart of his engine like a matador jabbing the sword between the shoulder blades of the bull.

As if he's practiced it a few times in his dreams, Danny does everything right, dodging the big hits by the other cars, flooring his car backwards into the steaming front ends of near unrecognizable Tauruses and Bonnevilles. The low-pitched sound of the impacts startles her each time, like a mortar shell going off beneath the grandstand.

She captures everything on videotape, her fingers in a tense grip on the cool metal of the tripod, and finally it's down to two steaming hulks duking it out like huge metal heavyweight boxers in the twelfth round. The two gasping beasts circle around each other for a moment on their wobbling wheels, then circle again, and to her it looks like a bizarre dance. For a split second, she thinks music could be playing. Suddenly Danny floors the Fury backward for the coup de gras, his chrome pipes snarling with a last white-smoke roar. He hits the other raised-nose car squarely in the front, and the left front tire and radiator burst at the same moment with a quick guttural pop followed by a hissing sigh. The fans roar, and some of them stand up for car 777, dumping empty nacho baskets and Miller Lite plastic bottles to the grass below the bleachers. Dazed for those few seconds after it's over, she doesn't know if she applauds or screams or just sits silently.

What she does get is a close-up of him though the lens, standing on the roof of the car, holding his gleaming trophy in the air. When the announcer interviews him after the race, asking what he's going to do with all that cash, Danny replies, to a round of chuckles and applause from the fans, "Buy another demo car." She hopes he won't park that 777 car on the lawn of the house later tonight, that he'll leave it at the track, at least for a while. She doesn't want to see its dented body up close, all those crater marks.

*　*　*

He's so excited about the win and his $500 cash prize plus the watermelon money that he can't stop talking about it over dinner. She listens quietly, with passive interjections like "Umm hmm," and "Yeah" and "Oh?" He doesn't seem to notice she's had enough of this conversation, that she needs it, right now, to take a different turn.

After dinner he hurries to the den to watch the videotape. He stays down there an hour, then two, as she sits upstairs, knees pulled up to her chin on the couch in front of the living room TV. She's not really watching any of the sitcoms that come and go every half hour; she's just staring in their general direction, letting their dialogue and canned laughter float past her.

*　*　*

By ten o'clock that evening, she knows what she has to do.

She strolls slowly down the stairway, crosses the den, and stands right in front of his TV set. She hears a waltz sliding through the speakers.

"Hey, look out," Danny commands from a few feet away, "I'm trying to edit this thing." But she doesn't move, just stands there staring at him as though she's turned to steel.

15

The Demolition Derby Driver's Wife

"What?" he says, raising his bushy eyebrows. "What?"

She lifts her arms toward him. "Come here," she says. "Take my hands."

He leans back against the couch a moment, stunned, as though he's just taken an unexpected hit to his side door, or as though he's somehow forgotten how to gently grasp her hands the way he did when they were first married.

For a few seconds, he stares at her, his numb face changing shape like a dent in a fender being slowly pounded out. She wishes she understood what was going through Danny's head right now. The thing about him is that she never knows what's going on inside that enameled shell of his.

What she *does* know for sure is that if he doesn't respond this time, she'll walk back up the stairway, grab the keys to her Malibu in the driveway, and speed away. Where she'll go, she's not sure: to the county highway, maybe. To a drive-in movie, where she'll sit without the gray speaker box hooked in her window, just watching the silent images of some love story on the screen. Or even to the Golden Spike, a couple miles out of town. Without even thinking, she might suddenly throw the car into reverse and then back the gleaming chrome rear bumper into the fender of that demo derby car parked alongside the fence. She'll hit it again and again, flattening it, flattening it, until number 777 isn't even recognizable as a car, until the metal is hammered thin as a sheet of paper. She stands there in front of the TV a few more seconds; the light from the screen flickering in the dim corners of the room. She hears the melodic instrumental playing behind the sounds of roaring exhaust pipes and metal crunching metal.

"Come here," she says again, her voice softer this time. Lilly begins a quick countdown in her head, giving him just a few more seconds. She wants him to do something besides staring at all this destruction; she wants him to catch fire, to glow like he used to.

Then, without a word, a slight smile scraping his face, Danny rises from the couch and glides toward her, reaching out stiffly as if he's about to take her in his arms, as if, even though it's a little clumsy, they're about to dance.

SKIP REMEMBERS
Fainting

We didn't know much then—what we did know were the insides of cigarette packages and the inside of the boys' room where, during recess, we sneaked in to try some fainting. There we were, Phil Keyhoe, Tommy Madsen, and me, Skip Carrigan: three cocky eighth-graders crouched on our haunches in the middle of the bathroom. We'd gulp in ten or twelve breaths, then stand up quickly, pinch our mouths shut with our fingers and blow hard into our taut cheeks until the blood rushed back into our heads and we'd faint.

It was a good way to spend time during recess that spring, we all agreed—a good way to forget Catechism lessons drilled into our heads by black-and-white nuns. The bathroom was an oasis of clean beige-and-aqua-tiled walls, gray metal stalls, and high, opaque windows so no one could see in or out. The urinals were always too white. We kept it quiet so Sister Agatha, with her hooked fingers, didn't discover us down there—she'd march us to see Father Francis for sure. We kept our talk to whispers that echoed off the polished walls of the room.

Somewhere that year, Tommy started stealing Kools from his old man. We'd slip between the moist, dark walls of the A & P and Cashman's Garage and we'd each smoke one. Near grade-school graduation we got braver and smoked them at dusk on the edge of the school playground. The orange tips glowed like fireflies. We took smoke as deeply into our lungs as we could and held it there, savoring the taste. Sometimes Phil would smirk, then let loose that repressed chuckle, his laugh coming out in little bursts of smoke. Between puffs, and after we finished a cigarette, we'd eat the strawberry taffy we bought at the theater candy counter. We thought it disguised the smell on our breaths. We all agreed the strawberry taffy and the smoke tasted great together.

The first time we tried fainting, we took turns. Tommy was first. He gulped in the breaths, but nothing happened. He just ended up red-faced, then he strolled to the mirror to comb his slicked-back hair. It was my turn. I got dizzy, and my sight turned fuzzy for a second, but it didn't work for me, either. Then Phil crouched down on the floor in his blue short-sleeved checkered shirt. He stood up and blew hard against his cheeks until his gaunt face brightened. Then he began to slowly topple backwards. At first Tommy and I thought he was faking. But he kept falling stiffly toward the floor like a huge tree that had just been cut. I dashed over, caught him behind his bony shoulders just inches before he would have hit his head on the hard tiled floor. I held him there, and he was out cold a few seconds; his arms slid limply across his chest and the air exhaled from his lungs. When he woke, he didn't remember what had happened. Later we remarked that he almost cracked his damned skull wide open.

After that, we always made certain we had one fainter and the other two standing close by. Or we'd faint in Tommy's bedroom after school, where Tommy cranked up some rock music and we could fall on the saggy bed if we really passed out. We all got to like the feeling of fainting—that odd numbing buzz followed by the blackness that took us far from this world for a few seconds. Sometimes we had weird dreams, and the time always slowed down—the few seconds we were out always seemed like half an hour.

A kid in class told us he heard about a boy somewhere who made himself faint and never woke up again. Tommy said he could always see our eyes roll back into our foreheads just before we blacked out. We laughed about it.

* * *

We laughed. We couldn't have known that five years later, the summer after high-school graduation, Phil would be killed when a car hoist crushed him.

I often imagined the car hoist in Cashman's Auto Body lowering on Phil, the whole weight of a Chevrolet on top of it. I tried to block it from my head: that vision of the wisps of smoke being pressed from his lungs. I never wanted to look into Cashman's garage door again, as we often did on the way to grade school those mornings. We'd rub circles on the dusty panes and peer in, and it would be cool and dark and exciting in there: the gray skeletons of unpainted cars, the stacks of hazy windshields, the girlie calendars with smudged thumbprints on them.

* * *

Toward the end of that school year, we learned that trying to make ourselves faint was a sin, and so Phil and Tommy and I rode our bikes to the church together and confessed it, one by one, behind the sweaty black curtain of the confessional. Kneeling in the pews, we'd offer up our ten Our Fathers to the plaster statues on the altar. *Forgive me, Father, for I have fainted.* The statues never seemed to have any eyes—only opaque marbles, as if they, too, were staring at the back walls of their skulls.

One time Phil and I were altar boys at a funeral, and we watched a woman in the front row faint dead in the aisle. The pallbearers had to lift her stocky body and lug her all the way up the aisle of the church with her gray dress riding up her thigh and her slip showing. Later, pulling our cassocks over our heads in the sacristy, we talked about it and snickered.

* * *

Tommy's a policeman in town now, and I don't get together with him any more. I only see him at church once in a while with his Marlboro pack showing through his white shirt pocket; he nods without smiling.

Once he mentioned that his job keeps him busy—he said I wouldn't believe the stunts he catches kids doing these days. We never mention Phil anymore, but I know from looking behind Tommy's eyes that he remembers.

Sometimes, when I'm driving around with nothing to do and I pass the old grade school, or when I'm filling the car up with gas or having my tires rotated, I still see Phil.

I see him teetering in his blue short-sleeved checkered shirt, see him falling backwards ever so slowly, his eyes rolling. And I always catch him just an inch from the hard tile floor.

20

MESMERIZING MINNIE

Another Life

Whenever I lean over the crystal ball, peering into its clear depths for secrets, I think of my mother. You might have heard of her—Estella the Teller, best traveling fortune teller this side of the Mississippi. She taught me everything I know—how to let my hands swirl like delicate clouds over the ball, how to open and close my eyes, fluttering my eyelids for effect, to hold my breath a few seconds as if going into a trance. But the one thing she didn't teach me before she left was how to find out about my own future. So far, no matter how long I stare, all I can see are those tiny bubbles suspended inside the cheap glass. So far I'm still holding my breath.

The customers, clutching their five-dollar bills, step tentatively through the tent flap like they're entering another world. They're nervous, as if they have the feeling they're wearing their skins for the last time and they're about to shed them in wrinkled piles in the corner. It's like a phone's been ringing for a long time deep inside their skulls, and they finally pick up the receiver and say, hesitantly, *hello*. They think it's me, *Mesmerizing Minnie, the Fortune-Teller*, but it's really their own voice on the other end of the line. "Sense them out," Mom used to say. "Figure out what they want. Then let them talk to themselves." Decent advice, in any profession. Stella was always like that. Practical, in a mystical sort of way. Giving people what they wanted. Trouble is, she never knew what to give herself.

For the last few years, I've been leaning over my crystal ball in the carnival. I know it's not real crystal—just glass made at a factory somewhere in Jersey. It's just ordinary glass, the kind you'd drink water from at a truck-stop counter. The only thing that's real for me in this job is the smell of oil-fried mini donuts and corn dogs that waft through my tent from the nearby concession stand. The only thing that's real is the scratchy midway music that plays from the paint-chipped metal speakers hooked on wooden posts. "Toot toot tootsie, goodbye," the song warbles, "Toot toot tootsie, don't cry," as the customers drop the fives into the fishbowl on my table, old Abe Lincoln smiling a little like the Mona Lisa, as if he knows something I don't.

The only thing that's real is that I miss my mother, but there's no way I can get her back. Not ever. Not where she's gone. I once heard a story about Harry Houdini. When he was lost beneath the ice of the Detroit River, holding his breath, he heard his mother's voice calling through a hole in the ice. And he survived because he followed that voice. But not me. Not Minnie Esmeralda. Lately it feels like I'm beneath a layer of ice, just swimming aimlessly for my life, the air in my lungs running out.

*   *   *

I remember, a decade ago, Stella teaching me the ropes. She said to back off just a little during the telling. "Keep one or two things cloudy, a secret," she told me. "They'll come back. If you're lucky, some people come back five, ten times," she explained. Maybe she *did* have a little magic, a little clairvoyance—I never really knew. One thing I was certain about her was that she could sway in her black sequined gown and make music. She had a knack for telling people their best choices, and people loved her, they *believed*. Belief—that's all you really need, whether you're teller or customer.

But Mom's own choices always shattered like cheap wine glasses. There was Ralph, a guy she left school for when she was a senior at Cosmos High. At first they were Bogie and Bacall and all that schmaltz. Or so she liked to think. The marriage lasted all of three months, but that was long enough to get me started. After that, there were flats we lived in until they raised the rent; there were houses she almost bought, small houses with gardens where she was on the verge of bringing me up in a nearly normal life; but then the banks got wise, checked into her phony account balances, and the deals fell through.

Cosmos was that kind of town for us. People always claimed it was the center of the universe, and a magical place, what with the town name and the streets called Milky Way Drive and Gemini Avenue, but that remains to be seen. One day at the library I looked up the town history in an old book and found it was really named after some drunken Frenchman named Jacques Cosmeaux, who founded the settlement during the fur-trading years and was eventually killed by the Indians after he raped the chief's daughter. The white settlers kept his name but, of course, Americanized it into Cosmos.

Anyway, my mom had jobs that lasted a while until the business closed or they cut back on help. Stella, with no diploma, was always the first to go. Early one summer, when she met a guy from Satellite Thrill Shows and Amusements—the carnival based in Cosmos—she got pulled into the carney life. The midway, the games with impossible odds, the blaring music, the World's Smallest Horse that sometimes bit the little kids, the Amazing Bird Child, Half-Human, Half-Bird, displayed in a jar, the rusting, creaking rides that made you dizzy—it all started to appeal to her because she fell in love with Ping-Pong Tony.

* * *

"We are about to go on an adventure," I remember Mom saying to me with a dramatic voice and a half smile. She was packing her suitcase and her cosmetic tote. I was only six then. "We will leave town for the summer with a tall, dark stranger," she continued. "We will start another life." She gestured vaguely in the air of our cramped apartment. "Are you excited, my Minnie?" I nodded. I believed.

I remember when Mom developed her act. A few weeks after we started traveling with the carnival, we were somewhere in Illinois when Tony, setting up the Tilt-A-Whirl with a wrench, sighed and wiped his forehead, then said to no one in particular, "Dammit, when will I ever get rich?" Then he looked into Stella's eyes and said, "Tell me the answer, baby. You look like a fortune-teller today." She just closed her eyes a few seconds like she was looking at the answer but wasn't going to say what it was. She always had that power.

The next thing I knew, she bought some strange gypsy duds at the local thrift store, including an old black scarf that she wrapped into a turban and bobby-pinned to her hair. She set up a card table in a small tent and got Splat the Clown to paint a sign—a cartoon of a fortune-teller. Splat was the artistic one among the carney crowd. He also was great at breaking into locked cars in the lot. Two weeks later, when the mail-order glass ball arrived from New Jersey, Estella the Teller was born. She invented her own chants, her incantations, her rituals, like dusting off the crystal ball with white chicken feathers before she began the reading.

It was fun at first. I got to play Teller's Assistant that summer, and it was my job to direct people into Mom's tent. Mornings, before the county fairs opened their gates, I was an ordinary second-grader, playing with Barbies and My Little Pony. *Minnie's so quiet*, the carnival workers said. But in the evenings, I took flight; I was Princess Minnie, dressed up in cheap robes, glitter in my hair, using an exotic low voice to usher people through the tent with a fluttering wave of my hand. It would have been a weird life for some people, but to me it was normal, and I loved it.

Sometimes, when I wasn't hanging around Mom's tent, I'd stroll down the midway to Tony's game. He wore a red-and-white pin-striped jacket while he ran the Toss-Em game, and in his breast pocket he always carried couple of cigars, which he never smoked. In his game, you threw ping-pong balls into open glasses that had numbers in them. I got to play it a lot for free, of course. If you bounced the ball into a glass with a blue number, you won a small prize—a key chain. If you landed it in the red shot-glasses in the middle—which you never did, Tony assured me—you got a big prize like a stuffed teddy bear with eyes that rolled around inside those clear plastic circles. After quite a few tries, I realized Tony was right. Though the ball sometimes bounced near, it *never* landed in the middle glasses. Maybe there was cellophane over them anyway. Tony handed me the gaudy pink key chain, shaped like a circus elephant, which I fastened next to the row of other key chains on my belt.

Other times I'd stroll down the midway to look at the Amazing Bird Child. I'd stand in front of that display case, clutch the velvet rope that kept the crowd back, and stare at the Bird Child in a gallon jar filled with formaldehyde. The child seemed to have two flesh-colored wings on its back, about the size of a dove's. The boy or girl—no one knew for sure—was coiled in a fetal position, its eyes closed, head bent to its chest as if praying. The child's skin looked pale, transparent, almost, beneath the two mounted spotlights aimed at the bottle. I remember feeling sorry for the Bird Child, suspended there on display for eternity, people paying fifty cents to walk in and gawk at it.

One evening at closing time, I slipped into Mom's tent and she seemed sad, the way she stared down at the vinyl top of the card table. She'd already packed her crystal ball away in the wooden box with the velvet lining.

"What's wrong?" I said.

"Tony's going to leave me," she blurted.

I didn't know what to say. I didn't know Ping-Pong Tony very well. He always seemed to pay a lot of attention to Mom, so I wondered why she'd say that.

Mom and I walked down the midway back to our trailer. The next thing I knew, I saw Tony, standing in the narrow space between the concession buildings with this blonde woman, who, my mom told me later, was Evelyn the Snake Charmer. Tony didn't see us but we saw him, leaning close to her and kissing the side of her long, thin neck as she giggled. I could see Mom's eyes catch fire, even beneath their dark brown color.

Tony was gone the next morning. His Toss-Em game sat empty all weekend. The front of the stand was roped off, a piece of paper taped to it, the fancy hand-lettered words *Closed for Remodeling* written on it. Splat the Clown's handiwork, I figured.

That night, before she went to sleep, Mom lay on top of her bedspread and talked to me, and it was as if she was talking to herself. "Maybe I've lived another life," she said wistfully, "Maybe I was once in a queen's court. I was royalty, and I sat on satin couches and ate fruit all day and had all the lovers I wanted. So in this life, I'm paying for it."

"Don't worry, Mom," I said. "It'll get better." I didn't really believe it, I just thought I should say it.

"You're too sweet, Minnie," she replied, taking my hand. "It's all those sno-cones and cotton candy. They're making you too sweet." She pulled me close and hugged me. "And I want your life to be sweet, too," she said, beginning to sob. "I want a better life for you. Not this."

"I *like* our life," I said. "It's good. I don't *need* another life."

* * *

Mom stayed with the carnival even though Tony was gone. A few years later, by the time I was seventeen, Mom already had the cancer. It was filling her slowly, and she didn't even know it. After she got diagnosed, that summer after my high school graduation, we left the carnival and returned home. As I sat in the hospital near her bed those last months, Mom talked about herself as a little girl. She described her childhood, the daughter of proud Mexican-Americans on a farm outside Cosmos. She described the soft brush of the swaying fields as she ran through them barefoot. She described the chicken hawks, floating overhead in one spot, like kites attached to strings. She described the wind, and the way it felt so clean on her face.

"That was my other life," she said. "Not in some queen's court. Just free and young, walking through those farm fields here in Minnesota, watching the chicken hawks, feeling those corn leaves brushing against my legs when the wind blew." Then, for a few seconds, her eyes seemed to look inward. "I'm sorry, honey. Sorry for what I didn't do for you." She gazed at me through her tears. "You're a young woman already. And what have I given you?"

"You gave me a lot, Mom." I said, my voice cracking. "You did fine."

"In another life," she said with a faint smile, "things will be better for you. They'll be a lot better."

I wanted to scream at her: *What if there is no other life, Mom? What if there's only one chance?* But I just pinched my lips shut.

Then she looked at me, like she often did, as if she had something else to tell me, an answer of some kind, perhaps, but wasn't going to say it.

The next morning, the cancer took her.

Today I've been awake since four a.m., tossing and turning, remembering. At six o'clock, I walk outside, and my feet carry me through the back entrance of the fairgrounds on the outskirts of Cosmos. I walk past the frozen rides—the ferris wheel and Rock-O-Planes, which sit like steel skeletons against the sky. I pick up the vague scents of axle grease and funnel cakes and the jelled cotton candy some kid dropped to the packed dirt. Then there's the scent of formaldehyde, preserving this place from the outside world. It's too lonely here, I think, too quiet. I try to imagine the hawking calls, the squawk of the sideshow speakers, a scratched voice repeating *You simply will not believe it.* I pass the games on the midway, old Splat the Clown's booth where he still robs people who try to knock down those three wooden milk bottles. The odds are always weighted against you.

I untie the cloth straps that seal the Fortune-Teller tent, and step through the flap hesitantly. I notice a bobby pin—the kind my mother always used to wear in her hair—on the floor. I pick it up and squeeze it in my palm. At that moment I feel like my heart is a balloon, and someone is trying to pop it with a dart.

I sit down at the table, click on the desk lamp, pull the crystal ball from its black wooden box. It looks different in the dim light—it's like I could look far inside it, as if it wasn't a ball at all, but a tunnel to somewhere. As I peer into it, I think I see a small girl, run-

Another Life

ning through a rural field, her legs swishing through the soft, tall grass. I blink my eyes, blink them again, as if waking from a dream, but the vision doesn't change. I wonder for a moment if it's my past, or my future, or neither. And then the clouds begin to appear inside the ball. They rise slowly, at first, like billowing cream poured into a cup of coffee. The ball turns opaque and that's when I stand and return the ball to its velvet-lined box.

Outside the open tent flap, the heavy gray covers the sky like a layer of ice. I still have time, and I know where I have to go.

I walk quickly to the shed at the edge of the lot, pick up a rock and break the padlock from the back door. I step inside and there it is: the Amazing Bird Child, its wings slightly folded, floating in its vague, hazy liquid. It looks ridiculous on the shelf with no spotlights to illuminate it. I lean closer. The creases in the child's face make it look doll-like, plastic, like it was made in someone's basement. But I'm not sure.

I lift the jar and carry it outside the exhibit. *No more holding your breath, Kiddo,* I say, like I'm talking to myself. I balance the gallon bottle in front of my face a few seconds before I let it go and it drops in slow motion to the hard asphalt. When it hits, the glass shatters with a sharp sigh and the water drains, forming a huge dark puddle. I lift the child, carry its tiny, stiff body to the soft dirt near the fence. I dig a hole with my fingertips, then lower the child into it and cover it up.

For an instant, I think I hear my mother's voice whispering. Or is it just the rustle of the long weeds, blowing in the wind on the other side of the fence? What matters is that I believe. What matters is that, for one moment, half-child, half-bird, I believe.

As I pass the Fortune-Teller tent, I have the feeling that I won't be coming back here again. I reach beneath the rickety table, lift the black wooden box that holds my mother's crystal ball, and carry it from the tent. I won't be needing the crystal ball anymore, not where I'm going, but something tells me that I should have it with me, just in case.

28

SKIP REMEMBERS
Speedy

I really don't know what to say about Speedy except that he was assistant manager of the StarLight Theater, he stood four feet eleven inches tall, he had two thumbs on his right hand, and he walked faster than any person I'd ever known. On Friday and Saturday nights, Speedy's job was to patrol the raucous aisles of the StarLight Theater to keep the peace. But there was no peace in that theater; from day one, my best buddy Tommy and I declared war on Speedy. Whenever we started clapping at the wrong moments during the movie, whenever someone would crawl under the girls' seats, or belch loudly, or throw popcorn at the backs of the heads of the young marrieds, Speedy would rush down the aisle in his wrinkled navy suit two sizes too large for him, his arms swinging high at his sides, fast-motion pendulums. He'd pause in the darkness on his short legs and stare up and down the rows of junior high boys, our big feet propped on the red velvet seats in front of us. Sometimes, trying to look official, he'd pace back and forth at the very front of the theater, a rumpled silhouette dwarfed by the black and white heroes on the tall, bright screen behind him.

When Tommy and I were thirteen, we never knew what movie was playing. We'd heard the townspeople say that the Cosmos theater was some kind of historic place, what with its purple velvet curtains, its crystal chandelier, its tall gold pillars, opera-house box seats on the second level, and paintings of cherubs on the ceiling. Built after World War I, it was supposedly patterned after some fancy palace in Versailles. But we didn't care about that. All we cared about was that it was a Friday night, the end of another dreary week of junior high, and we had finally made a jailbreak from our houses and our parents. All we cared about was that we had a handful of Sour Tarts or Sugar Babies, which we bought from the orderly rows of candies while we scratched the glass of the candy counter with our quarters. All we cared about was that we had a couple of New Year's Eve noisemakers beneath our jackets to interrupt the love scenes and a few Kool cigarettes in our shirt pockets—stolen from Tommy's old man—that we'd light up in the narrow alley after the show.

We'd snicker when Speedy hurried toward us in his perfectly shined shoes, holding a flashlight that sent a weak yellow beam down to the sticky red carpet of the aisle. We loved it when we saw his tiny third thumb as he pointed at us and said, trying to sound authoritative, "Settle down. You settle down now." We'd just laugh and point back, proud of our normal hands. We'd have a standoff with him, mocking that intent stare on his narrow face, the pellet-like eyes set too closely together beneath his high forehead as he squinted, trying in vain to make himself look tough with his wrinkled navy suit and his hair slicked back and shiny in some out-of-it '40s style. It was impossible for any of us to judge Speedy's age in that suit—he might have been only twenty-five, but he might have been as old as fifty. "Doesn't matter how old he is," Tommy would say, settling the issue. "The fact remains that he's a creep."

Sometimes, as Speedy retreated from our row, tugging at his wide lapels, Tommy followed him up the aisle, imitating his bobbing walk. He told us later that he never could catch up to him. One Friday night in the theater, Speedy kept pacing back and forth in the front like a shooting-gallery penguin. On a dare from Tommy, I pelted Speedy in the back of his square head with a crumpled-up Milk Duds box. It was a long throw, about fifteen rows down the center aisle, and I couldn't believe I actually hit him. But in the middle of two lovers kissing on a rerun of *From Here to Eternity,* the box struck Speedy's head with a flat sound. *Thwack.* The sound echoed across the high walls of the theater. Giggles broke out everywhere in the audience.

Speedy spun around, infuriated, and glared at the row of us guys. I looked right into his eyes as he approached—a trick I learned from Tommy—and Speedy never even suspected it was me. He just shifted his gaze down the row to the red-faced boys, muffling their laughter, their eyes fixed straight ahead at the screen.

The next week at school, Tommy brought his Dad's oversized sport coat and, with the guys gathered around him in the hallway, he did a hilarious impression of Speedy whirling around after he was hit by the Milk Duds box. Tommy did the routine over and over, and the guys laughed until they cried.

That year, Tommy claimed to me that we were going to grow up to look just like James Dean and have a babe like Marilyn Monroe or somebody leaning over us with a long milky cleavage. Tommy always said that she'd be something like the woman wearing that low-cut dress who sat behind the cloudy glass of the theater ticket booth. Tommy often remarked on her pouting red lips; he said she was really good-looking for someone from the crummy town of Cosmos, and that she probably should have tried out for the movies. We'd stare dreamily at her cheekbones jutting out like smooth walnuts and her bosom overflowing from her dress.

In eighth grade, we were still getting into the theater on the cheap fare. When we stood in front of the ticket booth, Tommy would mutter "Two children" through the hole in the glass.

"Children?" she once questioned in a soft voice. "Children are twelve and under."

"Yeah," said Tommy confidently. "We're twelve and under."

She'd shake her head and lean forward in that dress and press a button on her desk for the kid's tickets, which were a buck cheaper than the adult fare. With a hiss, each ticket slid like a frayed paper tongue out of the slit in the metal counter.

"Think she likes me?" Tommy said once as we lowered ourselves into the seats. Tommy and I figured she was at least twenty-five. When I gave him a questioning look, he said "Alice. The woman in the booth."

"How should I know?" I said, tossing a handful of popcorn into my mouth as Tommy ate alternately from his Sweet Tarts and Sugar Babies.

That spring, the girls in our junior-high classes snubbed us; they always seemed to look the other way whenever we'd brush past them in the hallways or at the soda fountain. So Tommy and I decided we were tired of all the junior-high girls in town. We knew them all too well, with their cashmere sweaters and their cheap little jewelry and their bobbed hair, and that familiarity soured us on them. We'd stand there at the dance at the junior-high gym, our arms crossed as we leaned against the shiny varnish of the folded-up bleachers. We watched the older couples dance beneath the crepe paper streamers of a ceiling that, as if it was breathing, seemed to rise and fall every few seconds. Tommy always summed it up best when he and I finally walked out of the gym after not even dancing once: "These girls are nothing, man. Nothing. Things are gonna happen for us, Skip. Just wait. You just wait."

And we did wait. We waited a long time. We figured we'd eventually meet some *real* girls at the high-school teen dances at Portage or North Freedom, two nearby towns. We figured we'd meet some *real* girls out at the lake or at the quarries next summer. We might have to lie a little about our age, Tommy told me, but so what?

"They'll see us for who we really are," proclaimed Tommy.

"So who are we?" I asked.

Tommy lit up a Kool as we got to the edge of the school grounds, tipped his head back and said, "The next James Deans, you dope. Who the hell else?" Tommy sometimes talked about going to Hollywood. He must have had rugged good looks, at least judging by the way out-of-town girls at the lake always looked at him and giggled, which we both took as a very good sign.

One night after school, as we stood in the alley behind the theater, Tommy inhaled the smoke from his cigarette, exhaled some words slowly. "My Mom and Dad fight all the time." He paused. "Now they're talking about getting a divorce." He said the words flatly, as if reading an assignment for a math problem he didn't understand.

"Really?" I said, blinking at him. I never knew anybody whose parents were divorced.

"Probably never happen," he said, tugging at the tatters on the wrist of his older brother's blue and gold letter jacket.

The next night at the theater, before the feature started, they played the same ancient song they had played for years: a scratchy version of "I've Got the World on a String." Tommy brought along a pocketful of small steelie marbles in his letter jacket and started firing them at the screen, where they landed with a dull *thump* that seemed to dent the faces of Audrey Hepburn and Carey Grant. In less than five seconds—we timed it—Speedy came scurrying down to scout out the situation.

After a moment of staring up and down the aisles, he retreated, scurrying under the gold-leaf archway in the back. Then an ominous shape in a iron-gray suit appeared, his bald head glowing beneath the archway light; and suddenly, like it was moving down the rows in a wave, you could hear the creak of the seats as kids straightened their backs and whispered the one word that struck fear into our guts in that theater. "Baldy," they'd whisper. "Cool it, you guys, it's Baldy."

Baldy was the manager and owner of the theater, a tall ex-Marine, and he was only called upon during the severe disruptions, like the time one of our friends and some town tough guy actually got into a fistfight. When Baldy appeared, we knew it was an extreme measure; we knew that we were on dangerous ground. Unlike Speedy, if there was the slightest hint of trouble, Baldy would yank on our arms and throw us out without giving us our money back. If Speedy was the Court Jester of the StarLight Theater, then Baldy was the Executioner. We all stared straight ahead at the screen as Baldy stalked down the slanted aisle, his head pivoting smoothly left, then right, as if it was on greased ball bearings. Nobody dared laugh or snicker. As he paused by our row, the whole theater seemed to take a deep breath and hold it in.

"You!" Baldy called, pointing to Tommy. Tommy looked up at him, wide-eyed and a little scared, and I felt a numbness rushing across my skin. Baldy had obviously gotten the word from Speedy about who was throwing at the screen.

"Me?" Tommy said innocently, pointing to himself.

"Yes, you," Baldy repeated, "Get over here." Out of the corner of my eye, I saw Tommy take his last couple of steel marbles—hidden inside his Sugar Babies' wrapper—and toss them into his mouth. Tommy stood and slid past our shuddering knees to the aisle.

Speedy, relieved to have reinforcements, appeared behind Baldy like a squat shadow, folded his arms, and watched the proceedings, a smug half-smile dabbing at his small lips.

"Were you throwing something?" Baldy demanded. He shined his flashlight beneath Tommy's chin, and the weird play of light and shadows made Tommy look much older. "Arms out to your sides," Baldy ordered. He began to frisk him, checking all his pockets. "What did you throw at the screen?" Baldy jabbed his thick finger into Tommy's striped shirt.

"Noshing, shir," Tommy slurred through the mouthful of steelies. The scene was comical, but none of us dared to burst out with a laugh.

Then Baldy scrutinized him, aiming the flashlight right up to Tommy's jaw as if the light could pierce through it like an X-ray.

"What do you have in your mouth, buster?"

"Sugar Babies," I blurted.

Baldy's head turned toward me. I swear he wasn't human, and his head was attached on a mechanical swivel. "I didn't ask you," he barked.

He turned back toward Tommy. "Open your mouth," he commanded.

I saw Tommy swallow hard, and to this day I still think I heard the muffled click of the steelies in his mouth just before they slithered down.

34

He opened his mouth wide for Baldy, who peered in with the flashlight. I saw Speedy, on tiptoes, craning his neck to see over Baldy's shoulder and into Tommy's mouth.

"Do I have any cavities, Doc?" Tommy quipped.

"You sit the hell down and watch the show," hissed Baldy. Speedy concurred with a nod. "And if there's one more bit of trouble from this row," added Baldy, "I'm throwing the whole bunch of you out." Baldy made a quick military turn, glanced at Speedy, and said through his teeth "Next time you handle this yourself." Then he strode back up the aisle, leaving Speedy standing alone, surrounded by the rising tide of our nervous snickers.

After the show that night, in the back alley behind the theater, Tommy stood beneath the black fire escape with his collar up and lit up a cigarette. We talked and smoked, and I guffawed as Tommy did an impression of Baldy's inquisition.

Then Tommy went silent a moment. He lowered his head, toed the cinders with his tennis shoe, told me that it was final—his parents really *were* getting a divorce. He told me he'd probably be moving with his father somewhere, maybe into an apartment on the other side of town.

"Does it bother you?" I asked.

"Nope," Tommy answered, "not really." Somehow I knew he was acting when he said that. He chuckled about the steelies again. "Shit, I really pulled one over on old Baldy," he said. "Didn't I?"

He added that he had a little stomachache from the steelies, but that was all. "But damn that Speedy for ratting on me," he sneered. "I hate that little jerk. He's gonna pay. I swear it."

On Saturday night, Tommy got the idea to wait until the theater closed, then follow Speedy home to see where he lived, maybe toilet paper his yard or something. We told the other guys about the plan; they all loved the idea and dared us to go through with it. So, at eleven thirty that night, after the last show let out, Tommy and I took off from our lookout post in the doorway of the soda fountain and tailed Speedy, staying about a block behind. We both clutched rolls of toilet paper we'd stolen from the theater bathroom, and we heard the guys behind us cheering us on. Speedy strode through the

35

downtown, past the big clock tower on city hall, and past the looming grain elevator across the river bridge on Main. "Jesus, that little sucker's fast," panted Tommy with a grin, as we followed about a half block behind him. Beneath a streetlamp, Speedy took a crisp left turn into the dingy trailer court—Royal Oaks Estates—at the edge of town.

After he entered the tin door of a rounded pink-and-beige trailer at the back of the court, we dashed across the dirt parking lot. We bent low as we tiptoed up to Speedy's trailer, then peered in through the small, dust-caked side window. Speedy had a wife who was twice his size; she stood in a faded floral dress in a room with two Formica end tables and a small sofa. On the maple paneled wall, near the ceiling, hung a picture of an ocean scene that we recognized from Woolworth's.

"So how'd it go?" she asked with a husky voice.

He shrugged. "The usual," he said, his voice, high and twanging like an announcer at an auction. He slid off his suit jacket, tossed it to a chair, and stood in his white shirt and red-and-navy striped tie. He actually looked a little younger without the jacket, and a little shorter, too, as if that were possible.

"What happened to your new shoes?" she asked, pointing down at Speedy's black shoes.

"Aw, somebody dumped a cup of pop on them."

"Those damn kids," she snapped, shaking her head. "Mr. Schultz doesn't pay you enough down there. Not for what you go through every week."

Speedy didn't reply, just took a deep breath as if inhaling all the air in the trailer.

"Better clean those shoes, Herbert," she commanded.

Herbert? the name reverberated inside our skulls. Everyone had called him Speedy for as long as we could remember, but he actually had a name—and his name was *Herbert.* We glanced at each other, holding in our laughter until it hurt.

He turned to the kitchen, which was only a couple feet away, pulled a frayed towel off a rack and dampened it beneath the faucet in a small porcelain sink. He lifted his shoes, one by one, onto the dinette chair with a yellow plastic seat cushion and wiped off the sticky pop. Then he turned toward his wife and reached out to hug her. His pendulum arms were motionless around her thick, bulbous waist. Speedy seemed to be swallowed whole for a second, and then she pushed him away.

Crouched there, Tommy and I suddenly felt embarrassed, paralyzed in the light from the trailer window, afraid to keep watching, afraid not to. I glanced at Tommy and noticed a strange look in his eyes as the yellow light struck his face brighter than any flashlight.

Then Tommy finally broke the trance as he whispered hoarsely "Let's get out of here." The next thing I knew we were both running across that dirt parking lot and toward downtown. As we ran, neither of us admitted it, but we were both sorry we had ever followed Speedy home and spied on him in his dingy trailer house. Neither of us said it, but somehow we both knew that, after that night, things wouldn't be the same with Speedy. As we crossed the Main Street bridge, Tommy tossed the rolls of toilet paper over the iron railing and we watched them fall toward the river, soft white flares with long, unraveling tails.

*　　*　　*

Before classes on Monday morning, I saw Tommy standing by his locker. I figured he'd probably tell some of the guys, cackling between words, about Speedy's dumpy trailer, about his fat, ugly, three-hundred-pound wife who bossed him around. I envisioned an even bigger group, gathering near Tommy beneath the flashing bulbs of the theater marquee on Friday, as Tommy would retell the story, acting it out with a little more flair this time as Speedy's wife grew to five-hundred pounds, until she tipped the whole trailer down on one end like a teeter-totter. I pictured the guys laughing and laughing until their stomachs hurt and they had to bend over from the sheer joy and pain.

But before school that day, Tommy surprised me when the only thing he mentioned was the earth science quiz we'd have during fifth hour.

"Hey," one buddy asked as he shuffled past. "You follow Speedy last weekend? Find out where he lives?"

As more of the guys crowded around, Tommy hesitated, glanced quickly out of the corner of his eye at me, then back at them. "Aw, we followed him a couple blocks," Tommy finally said. "But not all the way home."

"Why not?" one guy demanded.

"You know Speedy," Tommy chuckled, "he was too damn fast for us. We couldn't keep up with him. Right, Skip?" He elbowed me in the ribs.

"Right," I nodded, figuring maybe Tommy just wanted to wait for the right moment to tell the whole story.

* * *

But Tommy never did tell that story. Before the next show, a group of us guys hung out, and all Tommy talked about was the ugliness of the town streetlights and how he'd like to bust all of them with a rock one of these fine nights.

When it was time to go in for the movie, the rest of the guys bought their tickets ahead of us. Tommy and I stepped up to the cloudy glass of the ticket booth, and Alice, in her usual red dress, looked at him, twisted her mouth to one side, and said, "I know, I know. Two children." Her voice was chocolate syrup sliding down a scoop of ice cream.

"No," said Tommy. "Two regular tickets."

"Two adults?" she said, lifting her milky chin with surprise. "Just have a birthday or something?" Her full red lips parted for him in a smile.

"Yeah," said Tommy.

Her perfect hand pushed the tickets through the small arch at the base of the glass, and she wished him a happy birthday.

"Now it's official," Tommy announced as we slid onto the slashed velvet seats, "she *does* have a crush on me."

* * *

Tommy and I sat in our row in the dimness of the StarLight Theater, and I don't remember exactly what happened during the movie that night. Tommy probably ate alternately from his box of Sour Tarts and his handful of Sugar Babies, as usual; he said that the

Small Dances to an Unheard Song

candy always gave him a stomachache, but he ate it anyway. I'm sure Speedy made his rounds that night, and some of the kids probably mocked him. What I do remember most is that after the show, we lit up a couple of Kools in the cramped space between the theater and the old two-story hotel. Tommy took a deep drag, and with the kind of squint you get when smoke stings your eyes, he told me his Dad was looking for a better job, and they were moving out west next week.

"We're probably heading to California," he sighed, opening the wrinkled bag of Sugar Babies, which he always saved so he could eat some between drags of his cigarette. "That's what my old man keeps saying."

Tommy and I had been best friends since kindergarten, and it bothered me a lot to think of him leaving. I didn't know what to say, so I just stared down at a crushed cigarette butt, nudged it with the toe of my shoe.

I watched him pace back and forth a few times, and when he paused, silhouetted in the shadows, he looked suddenly smaller. He shook the last couple of candies out of the bag, offered me one, then ate the rest.

"Who knows," Tommy finally said, a half-smile smearing his face, "the old man and me might end up in Hollywood. Maybe you can come and visit. I'll show you around."

"Sure," I said, though I doubted that would ever happen.

"Hell, you might just see *me* on the silver screen some day." Tommy hunched over, did his quick James Dean impression, and I mustered a chuckle, though we both knew Dean had been dead for years.

Then he reached into his jacket pocket, pulled out some steelies. "I still got a couple of these left," he said. "You might need 'em this year."

"Naw," I said with a wave of my hand.

For a few seconds, I pictured Speedy rushing up and down the noisy aisles during the second feature, his short legs trying in vain just to keep up with the endless pranks. Pictured the younger kids in the lower grades, just catching on about how to get Speedy's goat. I didn't know what Tommy was thinking. We had a habit of that, both of us feeling things churning deep inside us, but neither one able to reach that far down and pull the words out. So we just leaned our bony shoulders against the crumbling brick wall and gazed up between the buildings at the pale clouds of exhaled smoke that rose and disappeared in the narrow strip of night sky.

GERALD, THE RETIRED SCIENCE TEACHER

The Things That Are Close, A Story of Love

When I was younger, I dreamed of saving the world. I used to lie in bed in the middle of the night, staring toward the plaster ceiling, though I couldn't see it, and think about finding a cure for cancer or discovering the key to genetics or solving the problems of world hunger. But now that I'm older, I don't think about those things. Instead, I spend my time peering through a telescope on the third floor of my house. It's been a long time since I've thought about saving the world—those dreams seem distant now, like the furthest corners of the galaxy, and I wouldn't even know how to begin to reach them.

So instead, I study the stars.

I study the galaxy, its slow swirl. I study the universe, its dimensions from end to end.

For years, as a high-school science teacher at Cosmos High, my job was to teach equations, to hold in my hand a piece of paper with the answer, the solution. My objective was always precise: I calculated, I proved, and I wanted my students to do the same. Facts are what's important, I always told them, and myself as I drank my morning coffee—black, no sugar—in the teacher's lounge. Conclusions. Nothing more or less. It was the precision I liked, the satisfaction of finding the correct balance of an equation, the teetertotter unmoving, level. Certainty is life, I'd been telling myself for years, and life is certainty.

* * *

Lately I've been I studying black holes.

I study those areas in deep space that pull in all the light and nearby matter. You can actually locate a black hole through a powerful telescope, and you can calculate its size through a series of formulas. Scientists claim that a person might actually survive a trip into a black hole. Like dust drawn into a vacuum cleaner, they might enter it, then be pushed out the exhaust to some other universe. Most black holes are huge, but I was amazed to learn that some black holes are tiny, only inches in diameter. I imagine them being a keyhole leading into another world.

Thirty years ago, in my world of teaching, I was an ordinary science teacher in a slightly tight gray suit-jacket. I reported for work each morning at 8:12. In the teachers' lounge, I poured myself a cup of coffee, watching that stream pour from the spout of the aluminum bin and into my white porcelain cup with **I Love Science** on it, a red heart representing the word love. It always took exactly five seconds to pour that cup of coffee in the morning. Exactly five seconds.

Now, in retirement, I sleep during the day, when most other people are awake. When the sun rises, when the sky's too bright for stars, I'm asleep. Now others are dreaming when I am most conscious, and I dream when most people are awake.

Lately I've been imagining what it would be like to pass through a black hole. I picture myself in a small capsule, traveling at a terrific speed toward a spot in the distance where streaks of red and blue light are entering. I imagine the capsule shuddering, and I tip my head back and hear a high, whining sound that deepens to a roar. Suddenly it's dark. It's the purest blackness I've ever experienced—so dark, the darkness buzzes. My body is electricity, squeezed and rushing through a narrow black wire. I'm a millimeter thin and stretched a million miles long.

Then I push the thoughts from my mind; after all, daydreams are nothing more than the mind gone loose, without its harness. I glance at the brass clock on the mantle, my retirement gift from the school— it's almost evening, time for me to begin my daily climb to the telescope.

I study the planets.

I gaze at the planets through my high-powered telescope and think about what I can learn from them: their rings of rock, their fiery hot surfaces, their icy clouds. They all orbit the sun, its massive explosions occurring every second. I think there's a secret about them, the way they dance around one another, never touching, always the same distance from their burning mother. Of course, some day—millions of light years from now—they'll all come back to her. Pulled by her strong gravity, they edge imperceptibly closer each year; eventually their surfaces will singe, then turn molten, then burn to ash as they fall into the sun's surface. Sometimes I picture it happening as easily as a gull's feather floating into the cauldron of a volcano.

43

There are times I find myself speculating too much. Ever since I've retired, I've been thinking too many distracting thoughts, and I've been trying to break myself of the habit. I have to concentrate, to do what I need to do.

So I study the moon.

Just after dusk, moonrise: the one lone moon in the absolute expanse, a pearl dropped and floating in a bottomless sea of tar. I sit in my makeshift observatory on the third floor of my house and study phases of the moon, the cycles and what creates them. Through the telescope I see the Sea of Tranquility, that place where the astronauts landed years ago, the place where they planted a flag in the lunar soil in 1969, the dust floating, in slow-motion, from their boots. They took samples, even hit a golf ball hundreds of yards, the ball floating as if it would carry forever. While our astronauts walked on the moon, back on earth our country was fighting in Vietnam. When I look at the moon's empty face, I feel suddenly lonely. *What did we discover up there?* I catch myself wondering. *What, after all, did we really learn?*

Lately it's too big for me to think about, this solar system with its ebb and flow, its waves and cycles. Sometimes after I watch the sky all night and I stand in my kitchen as it brightens with the dawn, I'm baffled by all those things that are so far away from me. I think about how much I could do for the world, but I don't know where to start. Then I wonder why I'm just one human being in the middle of it all, one odd human being—rinsing his empty coffee cup— ebbing, flowing into a life he doesn't understand at all.

Last night through the telescope I got a glimpse of a dust cloud, a hazy collection of dust particles, and I thought: *That's me. That's me in a few million years.* So today I try to concentrate on the small, the specific, the nearby, to focus on things that are closer. The things that are close will keep me from losing my concentration.

Tonight I don't think about the universe, the galaxies, the planets, or the moon. I think about our own earth. I focus on high and low tides, winter and spring, rain and drought, day and night. Then I consider even smaller things. Continents, mountain ranges. Countries, cities, towns, remote villages, fields. The one county highway that leads from Cosmos to the neighboring town.

I think about what I can hold in the palm of my hand.

I think about one ear of corn I saw yesterday as I glanced out the kitchen window behind my house and discovered it growing from the stray stalk beside the fence. An ear of corn: its rows even, its smooth, round yellow kernels that seemed to glow. One ear of corn outside the small window: it kept me focused at dusk, before the first stars came out. I leaned there, my open palms pressed to the glass. Before I climbed up to my observatory yesterday, the beauty of one single ear of corn kept me from going insane.

*   *   *

To multiply the ear of corn by thousands, by millions, I've been thinking today, *that would be the feat.* To feed the hungry with it.

That would be a conclusion worth reaching. The simple ear of corn, multiplied. The simple ear, multiplied simply, so that it would feed multitudes. Fields and fields of swirling leaves of corn. How right, how wonderful the world would be.

Today, for hours, I've been thinking not about the galaxies, not about infinity, but about one ear of corn.

* * *

I wake from my sleep, and look out my window and see the red pulse of sunset. As I get dressed, I daydream a few seconds—not about the black hole this time, but of walking through row after row of cornfields.

Dusk is settling like a fine powder of ashes outside my window, and it's time to pour my coffee into the chipped porcelain cup and climb the creaking circular staircase to my telescope. I focus on what I need to do; I can't dream right now. Not right now.

Everything narrows toward its conclusion. I know this. So this evening, I take a different path to my observatory, and instead walk through the yard behind my house. Then I follow the spiral stairs upward, taking each step slowly, one at a time. I climb, letting the stairs take me where I need to go.

I place the one ear of corn on the wooden table next to me. I tip my head back into the headrest and peer into the lens of the telescope.

Suddenly I see something I can't explain. For a moment I think I've spotted a new celestial body. It's a sphere within a sphere, with its bluish-green exterior, its black interior core.

Then I realize: the lens cap is still on, and I'm looking at a reflection in the glass of the lens. It's my own eye I'm seeing—a tiny little planet, clear and round as the face of a child, far away and so close at the same time. And right now, it's a place to begin. Right now, as it stares straight back at me, it's enough to see.

45

SKIP REMEMBERS

Otie, Fake Fights

Those warm August nights after high school graduation, we laid on our backs on the grass of the town square and gazed toward the sky beyond the illuminated orange face of the old courthouse clock. Time never seemed to move too quickly or too slowly; it simply passed without our knowing. Darkened cars roared by, windows rolled down, the Beatles' "Ticket to Ride" blaring from scratchy radios. A few of us guys propped elbows beneath our heads, stared listlessly across the street toward the soda fountain, and dreamed of girlfriends, of our big hands fondling their shoulders in the soft backseats of our cars. Some of us closed our eyes and saw visions of the last game of the football season, when our team—the Cosmos Thunderbirds—lost by a touchdown on the final play of the conference championship game.

At least once each Friday night, Bob Otie would turn his jaw to me, and say: "Hey, Skip, wanna fight?"

"You better believe it," I'd answer through clenched teeth.

We'd stalk solemnly to the middle of the courthouse square near the gray granite Civil War statue while the rest of the guys followed in a line. There, on a patch of dark green grass, Otie and I faced each other, glaring, and slowly pushed up our sleeves.

"Come on, buddy," Otie taunted, curling his hands into fists that bobbed in the air. "Come on." The football-shaped Most Valuable Thunderbird pin gleamed on the lapel of his blue and gold letter jacket.

Suddenly, on cue, I'd swing my fist, missing Otie's chin by a fraction of an inch, and Otie would smack his palms together for a sound effect, turn his head quickly to one side, and fall backwards on the grass. Standing up slowly, he'd shake his head. Then he'd lean toward me menacingly, rotating his hands up and down like pistons. He'd swing hard, just missing my chin, and I'd smack my hands and fall. The rest of the guys would surround us in a circle, egging us on, shouting and pumping their arms. The fight continued until, if we were lucky, it drew some looks from the senior girls who always sat on the brick courthouse wall, swinging their newly-tanned legs.

Once Otto Grosshans, who was closing up the Rainbow Café, spotted us and thought our act was real; he came puffing toward us, his white-shirted belly bouncing over his belt. "Hey, you fellas!" he shouted. "You stop that!" We threw another fast punch or two, timing the sound effects just right. Then, just before Otto reached us, Otie and I, best friends, burst into laughter and took off. The other boys followed us, and, as Otto swore at our backs, we all ran full speed across the courthouse lawn, down the narrow cinder alley, and into the darkness beyond the streetlight.

*   *   *

That fall after graduation, some of us got jobs, like working at the quarry or the Industrial Casing Plant by the river, where we spent all day staring at the machines that made casings for rifle bullets and mortars. Some of us, those with good grades and enough money, went on to college, grew our hair a little longer.

And some of us, like Bob Otie, got drafted. He had told me once that he didn't especially want to go into the army, but if he was called, he'd go and shut up about it.

In basic training, boys from our class practiced bayoneting dummies. Bob Otie wrote me a letter from South Carolina, which I flattened on the Coke-ringed Formica counter of the soda fountain and read aloud as the guys crowded around me. We chuckled as Bob told us how stupid he felt sticking bayonets into dummies that looked just like the tackling dummies we used in football practice.

* * *

For years, Otto Grosshans kept the same window display in the tall front window of the Rainbow Café on the town square. At the back of the window was a faded cardboard picture from the '50s of a bow-tied man and a poodle-skirted woman drinking coffee and smiling. In the front of the window, surrounded by pale, dried wings of dead moths, sat two five gallon jars filled with green olives that had been there ever since anyone in town could remember. The olives were arranged symmetrically so that each red pimento faced the outside of the glass. At the barber shop, Otto was often overheard saying to Ned: "The display's real popular with customers, so why the devil change it?" And Otto had a point; people in town marveled at the jars of olives—the way they were preserved in perfect, even rows. Sometimes, stirring their morning coffee in circles, spoons clinking against the porcelain, customers in the Rainbow Café would smile and nod toward the olives as Otto stood proudly behind the wooden counter in his broad white apron, his fist toweling the inside of a thick parfait glass.

* * *

Boys from our class, dressed in olive green, held M16s in their soft hands as they stalked the rice paddies and jungle trails.

Otie wrote a second letter from a place in Vietnam none of us could pronounce. He said he actually missed the ol' town of Cosmos, said it seemed a million miles away. He asked if we were still hanging around the town square on weekends like we used to. He wrote that, as they marched in their column some days, they heard

Small Dances to an Unheard Song

the B-52s overhead on their bombing runs. He added: "The guys over here call them Thunderbirds. Crazy, ain't it? Thunderbirds."

* * *

Back home, we heard rumors about how the county draft board would be calling more and more boys into the service. The draft-age boys who stayed in town that fall began to worry, though if you saw them on the street, they might act cool and mutter *No sweat.* When news of the first area boy to be wounded in Vietnam reached Cosmos, Harley Shuckle, editor of the town's weekly paper, *The Cosmos Freedom,* printed a small article on the back page about the boy. He added that the boy, from Eagle Bend, was recovering well, and that none of our hometown boys had been wounded over there.

Saturday nights in December, in the empty lot behind the Casing plant, boys parked with their girlfriends in the backseats of their cars, the heaters going full blast. They'd stuff their letter jackets in the back windows, run their palms down the girl's smooth shoulders. There were times when, suddenly, the boys would pull back for a moment to stare into the girl's eyes.

"Why are you stopping?" the panting girl would whisper. "What's wrong?"

"Nothing's wrong," the boys would mutter. "Not a thing."

* * *

Bob Otie and I took a wrestling class second semester of our senior year. We hated that wrestling class, with its smell of stale sweat embedded in the hard vinyl mats and the low-ceilinged concrete wrestling room, which was nothing more than a converted storage space in the basement of the high school. Coach Gino Lucia, the high school wrestling coach, spent six weeks droning instructions about classic wrestling holds. Near the end of the class, he taped a chart to the cement-block wall and paired up Otie and me for our final wrestling match. Our grade depended on that match—it seemed perfectly fair to Lucia that winners received an A for the class while losers got a C. Checking his stopwatch, Lucia raised his hand in the air as Otie and I faced each other. "Weddy?" Lucia called with his Elmer Fudd accent. "Wessle!" Otie and I wrestled energetically, going for quick takedowns, pulling frantic reversals on each other. Otie was strong, but I was quick, and the score mounted up rapidly until it was 20 to 18, and I was ahead. I knew Otie's pride would be hurt if he didn't win; after all, he made the all-conference football team for three years straight. "One minute weft," Lucia barked as we backed away, gasping for breath, and stood hunched, facing each other across the nosebleed-smudged mat. Suddenly, as we stared into each other's faces, neither of us could keep from grinning.

"Come on!" Coach Lucia shouted. "Mix it up, you two. This ain't no junior pwom."

I lunged forward, grabbed Otie by the knee and got a quick take-down. Otie spun a reversal and suddenly he pinned my shoulders squarely to the mat. "One!" Coach called, slapping his palm on the vinyl. Otie looked into my eyes, and then I could feel him let up slightly. "Two!" coach shouted. Otie let up even more, and I easily rolled him over and pinned him.

The next Friday night at the soda fountain, I told Otie I *knew* he had let me win. "Fair and square," Otie said, as he sat in his red madras shirt, sipping a cherry phosphate and staring straight ahead at the tiers of Slo-Pokes, Sugar Babies, and Milk Duds. "Fair and square."

*   *   *

50

In January, there were more reports from Vietnam, and we watched black and white soldiers slap through the broad leaves on the evening news as we ate our dinners. The country was changing, and our little town could vaguely sense that. But Harley Shuckle, the newspaper editor, had a policy against printing any AP wire photos of the conflict. And he never mentioned the war in his weekly editorials. What he did mention was the size of the snowdrifts near the First National Bank, the Women's Club's Friday smorgasbord at the church, the new production line opening up at the Casing plant, and the plans for next summer's town festival, Cosmos Space Daze.

We used to work for Schuckle when we were in grade school, de-livering *The Cosmos Freedom* on paper routes. Before we took off on our bicycles, we folded each copy of the paper in half, in half again, then tucked in the free end so we could toss them like Frisbees to the wooden front porches. It was a simple thing, folding the papers like that, but the news always got smaller that way. The world got smaller. Bob Otie said he could hit Mrs. Trestle's narrow front porch, bull's-eye, from the middle of Main Street. The ink from folding those papers always smudged our fingers. By the time our routes were finished, our hands were gunpowder gray. It always took a while, standing at home at our sinks in the early evening, to wash the ink off with Ivory soap.

*   *   *

The town elders didn't think all that much about a war going on. On Sunday mornings, on the way to church, they passed the Rainbow Café with its gallon jars of olives in the front window. It was amazing how the olives sat in perfect rows, green eyes that stared, unblinking, toward the courthouse clock. As the people walked by, they nodded, or simply shook their heads with a kind of awe.

*   *   *

One February morning, we heard that the first boy from our town had died in Vietnam.

He was Bob Otie.

A week later, a lot of us from his class stood at the cemetery, staring at the mound of dirt next to the grave. It was hard to dig the grave, they said; the ground was so frozen. Over and over, we repeated the story of how it happened. Outside a small village, Otie had kneeled with a flashlight at the opening of a tunnel. He'd searched a lot of them before without any problem, but this one was booby-trapped, and when he reached into it, the mine exploded. All afternoon I tried not to think of the impact striking him. Tried not to think of him falling backward on the grass, his jaw blown off. *Killed instantly,* someone said; *it happened so fast, he probably didn't feel a thing.*

51

*   *   *

Harley Shuckle printed an article about Bob Otie in the obituary section on the second page of *The Freedom,* with Otie's senior class picture balanced at the top of the column. Just a couple of paragraphs reported the circumstances, listed survivors. Just a hundred words, some smeared ink on thin paper that would turn yellow and brittle after a couple years, no matter how you tried to preserve it.

*　*　*

On Memorial Day that May, some of us guys chipped in and put a bunch of flowers on Bob Otie's grave at the cemetery. The granite gravestone—right from our own Rainbow Quarry—was polished and smooth, and the sun glared off it, making us squint. The flowers weren't real; the florist at Cosmos Gift and Floral assured us the imitation ones would look just as good and last a lot longer.

As I walked home, I noticed, in the backyards of our town, the overalls on the clotheslines billowing with the gusts of wind. The hollow legs inflated, climbing as though trying to pull loose from the clothesline. When the wind died down, the pant legs lowered slowly, like flags, then fell still and motionless again.

Harley Schuckle printed a story about the Memorial Day parade for the paper. At the parade's end, people tossed the wreaths and flowers off the Broadway Bridge and into the brown, muddy water of the river. I stood alone on the shore behind the Casing plant, watched the tangled flowers and ribbons floating downstream in our river's slow current.

But the big front page feature that week was about the town's first drive-through bank near the city limits. The economy was growing, everyone said, thanks to the new government contract at the Casing plant addition. Otto Grosshans, representing the Businessmen's Club for the groundbreaking ceremony, appeared on the front page in an underexposed picture, his smile frozen, the tip of his shovel pushed a few inches into a field where we once played football as kids.

The rest of that summer, we'd still meet on the town square occasionally, though, as time went on, fewer and fewer of the guys showed up. Those of us who did show up had little to say to each other. Some of us walked idly up and down the sidewalk in front of the Civil War statue, which always seemed to be pointing its gun in our direction. One or two of the guys mentioned Bob Otie, and then, trying to change the subject, they'd mention that championship game we lost senior year. "We should of won that damn game," they'd say with a half chuckle.

*   *   *

When I stroll across the high-school parking lot some Friday evenings, for an instant, out of the corner of my eye, I think I see Bob Otie, standing in the doorway behind the reflecting glass.

Then I picture him, hunched across from me on that gray mat in senior-year wrestling class, his face about to explode into a grin.

The wrestling mat darkens into the green grass of the courthouse lawn where he faces me beneath the glow of the streetlight. It's just after graduation again, and I see his pale fists floating up and down, his face half grimace, half smile. All the guys stand in a circle around us, pretending to egg us on. Suddenly I swing, my hand quick as light, just missing his chin with my fist. After the smack, he falls on his back on the grass, his eyes closed for a few seconds. Then he opens them, shaking his head groggily, rubbing his face, playing it perfectly. He stands and beckons to me, and I know his cues; he'll let me win this match. It's beautiful, and amazing to watch: no matter how many times he falls, he opens his eyes, he rises to his feet again. And though he rubs his jaw, I know he doesn't feel a thing.

53

MOLLY

Runaway

It didn't seem to take long at all before Molly found herself at an intersection in Nebraska, hundreds of miles from home. She thought about her hometown's city limits sign, that ugly, yellow-faced sign that tried, for a few seconds, to stop her from leaving, its little black numbers, **4,821,** glaring at her. When she pushed hard on the accelerator, Molly began to feel a lightness; the old Reliant felt as if it were rising slightly and the wheels no longer touched the cracked, uneven pavement. Her long brown hair swirled, lifting off her neck. Soon the sign was far behind her, shrinking, melting in the sun like a Popsicle, leaving a ridiculous pastel puddle on the bleached pavement. But today, as the flashing red light in the rearview mirror burned her eyes, she pulled the car to the shoulder, fearing that something was about to catch up with her again.

* * *

Molly can't explain why she ran away in the first place. She can't really answer that question. She can't tell anyone why, three days ago, right after her last class at the high school, she just threw a faded purple backpack in the backseat and took off. Inside the backpack was a pair of baggy khaki pants and an old blouse, but no mirror. She didn't want the mirror, or the glitter makeup or lipstick her mother gave her for her sixteenth birthday. She backed the Plymouth Reliant out of the driveway just before her parents were supposed to come back from their weekend getaway in Madison. Molly Hutchinson from the town of Nowhere, Minnesota didn't want to hear about the great time they'd had in Madison; she didn't want her mother to dangle her new string of pearls—a gift from her father—in front of Molly's face. They always seemed to have such a fun time on those weekend trips without her.

If she were pressed to give an answer about why she ran, she would probably say something flippant like, "Maybe because the road was straight, and the tires were round" and leave it at that.

* * *

Sometimes it's the leaving that counts, she told herself as she drove through the flatlands just outside of Cosmos—not the why, not the where, just the leaving. Sometimes it's just the turning of the steering wheel that counts, the gliding toward a county highway intersection and then turning left, not because you want to, or have a reason to, not because it means anything, but just because the intersection is coming at you fast, and you just have to decide.

* * *

She's so tall, and so big for her age, her parents had said all her life. They used the words to explain her to people, and, at the same time, Molly couldn't help but feel they were condemning her, too. No one in the family was *that* size at so young an age. Her petite mother, only five feet three, sometimes tugged at the bottoms of the slacks she bought Molly just a month or two earlier. "These are almost a little short and tight already," she'd say to Molly, as if that comment might make her stop growing so quickly. Her father said that someone Molly's size should play basketball. Molly tried basketball in gym class, but she was too gawky and clumsy to be good. Her father was a fanatic about college basketball, and each season he avidly watched his old alma mater, Michigan, on TV. Whenever her father spoke to her, he used a kind of patronizing voice, as if he didn't really believe what he was saying. "Just talk *to* me," Molly sometimes wanted to shout at him, though she never did. "Not at me, not about me, but just *to* me, like I'm a human being." She knew he meant well, but his words always sounded stiff, rehearsed, like they could be meant for anybody, like he could be talking to a client at his business who was inquiring about taking out a loan.

* * *

Molly thinks about how they all want you to *be* something. Your parents and uncles and aunts stare at you as though they're waiting to watch it happen, as if you're one of those tiny sponge-like toys they've added water to, and they're waiting for you to grow ten times your size, to hit your head on the ceiling like some stupid Alice. How could she tell them that sometimes she just wanted to shrink instead of grow—that she wanted to be a girl—not some too-tall, too-large woman, but a girl again?

She wanted so much to tell them that—and to tell them that she hated basketballs, their rising and falling, the way they always have to go through a hoop or they're worthless. She wanted so much to tell them what she felt, but instead she just pinched her mouth shut as usual, her thin lips slanted slightly to the left beneath what her mother called "those big, happy eyes."

"I had those eyes once," her mother said wistfully. "My eyes were just like yours."

"When?" Molly asked, leaning toward her, thinking her mother was about to confide in her, which she never did. "When was that, Mom?"

"Once upon a time," her mother said, avoiding her question with a kind of irritating baby-doll voice she sometimes used. "Just once."

* * *

Maybe Molly left because the road was straight and the tires were round, and because she was too big, and because her eyes were like her mother's, and those reasons were reasons enough.

* * *

Small Dances to an Unheard Song

When she reached Portage, she stopped the car at a Kwik Mart, pushed open the squeaking door to the women's bathroom, and purposely didn't look at herself in the mirror. She unzipped her backpack and pulled out her driver's license, her photograph with the smile thin as a pencil line. She threw it into the metal garbage can beneath the towel dispenser. She took off her designer jeans and silky shirt and draped them on the porcelain sink, its white gone to a gray color from so many dirty hands.

Then she reached into her backpack, slid on the old khaki pants that were too baggy and the worn oversized denim blouse. She pulled out a red and orange macramé scarf and wound it three times around her neck. From her purse, she grabbed some wet wipes her mother insisted she carry and, without looking in the mirror, wiped off her eyeliner and mascara and blush. She scrubbed every bit off. Rubbed her skin until it stung. "Too pale," she could hear her mom saying, "You need more mascara for your eyes, and for those lashes." Always giving advice, she thought, everyone always wanting you to be them, as if their lives were so damn perfect.

Before she left the bathroom, she rolled her cast-off clothes into a ball around her red candy-colored cell phone with the Madonna ring tone on it, then stuffed them all into the garbage can. *A slam dunk,* she thought. *A score. Two points for me.*

* * *

The next morning she woke at a county park when the sun angled through the side window. She didn't know what time it was. She had no watch, and the '75 Reliant, of course, had no dashboard clock. At the next town, she ordered breakfast at the Hardees' drive-thru, and, back on the road, she found a radio station. *Runaway train,* the hoarse voice sang as the radio faded in and out with static, *Never coming back.* She sang along with it during the chorus—it was an old song, but a good one. Then, after a slow boring hip-hop tune like the ones the girls in her class swayed to in their girly-girl outfits, trying to look so cool, a Green Day song burst through the speakers, the drums exploding like machine guns; she turned the radio up loud, louder, so it almost hurt her ears.

* * *

Nebraska Border Welcome Center 45 the sign announced. The Nebraska border seemed like something she had always wanted to drive toward. Not because it was a place she wanted to be, but because it was an invisible line that would put itself in front of her and, like every other line, she would just have to cross it.

When she pulled over in a small town that evening and checked into a motel, the old woman behind the counter didn't question her age. Molly was only sixteen, but with her long frame and sculpted cheekbones, she could be mistaken for twenty-one. No one questioned her age, and she checked in, just like that. On the registration card, she wrote her name as Sally instead of Molly. She hesitated a moment before filling in her last name—because she hadn't planned what to write—then glanced behind the counter, spotted the "Air-Conditioned" sign, and quickly scrawled *Condition* for her last name. It was that easy: thirty bucks, a fake signature and address, a room key on a plastic holder shaped like a cow, and she was a new person.

She switched on the TV. She would watch whatever she wanted, but she would not look in the mirror. She was her own person tonight. She wasn't just plain too-big Molly Hutchinson, she was someone else. She was Sally Condition, and it felt good to be that person, watching the commercials for Skittles and Miller Lite and Wendy's, switching off *Entertainment Tonight* so she wouldn't have to see the plastic smiles of Britney Spears and Jessica Simpson and Paris Hilton.

58

* * *

She recalled the day after school when her mother sat her down on the floral sofa in their freshly painted living room and told her she could open her first checking account. She asked Molly which girls in school were popular, who had boyfriends, which ones had the best figures, which brands of clothing she liked the best; then she said how fun it would be to take a shopping trip to the city to Saks Fifth Avenue. She told Molly how cute she'd look in low-rise jeans and a bare midriff. The things mothers talk to their daughters about. She asked Molly which brands she liked best, then sat there, waiting for an answer. She sat there a long time, staring at Molly, waiting for her to speak.

Molly didn't reply, just stared at the pattern on the sofa, the pinks blending into the blues, the fake flowers caught in Scotch-guard cloth.

The next day, Molly walked into the local Salvation Army Store and bought big, loose shirts, baggy khaki pants with a red stain on the thigh, and a military green trench coat two sizes too large with the name *Kent* printed in marker on the label. The frayed, multicolored scarf caressed her neck, and when she slid her feet into someone's old floppy black Sketchers, size nine and a half, they fit just right. Molly went home, stepped into the foyer, and saw her mother gasp at the way nothing she wore matched. That was Molly's answer. And her mother's answer was to rush over, gasping, and tear the scarf from her neck and wad it into a ball, make her go into the bathroom and take the clothes off, order her to get in the shower and wash herself. As if the clothes were dirt, pure dirt on her skin.

"We have the money," she remembers her mother repeating at dinner. "Your father owns a business, you know." As if Molly didn't know. She never asked where the clothes went, though she suspected they were tossed into the dumpster near the alley, all twelve dollars and forty-seven cents worth. She managed to rescue the Sketchers, which she found in the stainless steel garbage bin in the kitchen. The multicolored scarf, coiled at the very bottom, hugged her hand as she picked it up.

Molly could not have predicted that, the next morning, she'd find an entire wardrobe laid out for her on the sofa: Calvin Klein jeans and blouses, tight knit tops, dresses and skirts, fancy knit sweaters, and America's Top Model scarves she wouldn't be caught dead in. And who would have known that Molly would try on all the clothes, step in front of the hallway mirror with its gold frame, and tell her mother they were "fine, just fine." She slipped into each lie, one by one, and she wore them well.

* * *

Maybe she left home because the road was straight and the tires were round, and because she was too big and too tall, and because she hated the feel of Calvin Kleins on her skin.

* * *

She lay back on the bed and stared at the cracked motel ceiling. The only sound in the room was the vague rush of tires on the highway as the cars slid past, going somewhere, nowhere. She thought about the people back home, finding out she'd run away—they'd figure there was a boy involved. They'd talk. They'd think she'd taken off for a few days with a boyfriend—some black-leather tough boy, a wrong-side-of-the-tracker, shunned by the family and her big-business father. They might even imagine them, wrapped together in the sheets in some cheap motel. But they'd be wrong. There was no boy involved. "Don't stand so tall around boys," her mother once warned. "Relax a little. You don't want to date a boy who's much smaller than you. It's not done."

She liked a few boys in her class, but they'd have to wait until later. No matter what people back home might think, there was no boy. Right now it was just her, and the car in the yellow-lined number 3 parking space, and this motel room. And as she thought about all this, she felt that free feeling again, as if she were about to rise a few inches above the bedspread.

A while later, though she didn't realize she was tired, she closed her eyes.

She thought about the afternoon when she came home from school the fall of freshman year. "What do you mean, not trying out for basketball?" her father asked, his face looking disappointed, slightly befuddled. "You said you would. Why aren't you going to?"

60

She opened her eyes and glanced anxiously around the room. He wasn't there to scold her. She slipped from bed, clicked on the TV set, even though it was two-thirty in the morning. The latest Calvin Klein girl slinked in front of the camera with her wispy hair, her long legs gripped by those tight jeans.

Before Molly knew what was happening, she was out of bed, picking up the brass lamp from the nightstand. She lifted the lamp in front of the TV, wanting to throw it, base first, right into the face of the Calvin Klein girl, to shatter her into a thousand pieces. She held the wavering lamp there a few seconds, then finally tossed it hard to the floor, the Soft-White bulb shattering as she did.

She got dressed, grabbed her belongings, and drove out of the motel parking lot and into the darkness. As the Reliant cruised down the county road, she looked up and saw the moon, still nearly full. The moon was leaning its face over her, but it wasn't judging her. *The moon is whole*, she thought, her fingers shaking on the wheel. *Not a thousand pieces.*

*   *   *

Maybe she left because the road was straight and the tires were round, and because she was too big and tall, and because the Calvin Klein girl needed to be shattered into a thousand pieces. She would drive and keep driving. The road felt straight and whole as it whispered to her tires. What was it whispering? What? She leaned close to the dash to listen.

*   *   *

That's when she heard the sound. It wasn't the sound of the road; it was a sound of something rising and falling. Looking into the rearview mirror, she saw those flashing red lights right behind her. Her fingers went numb on the steering wheel. For the first time since she left, her body suddenly felt heavy, her wrists weighted down by lead sinkers. It was as if her body was sinking right through the floorboards of the car and into the pavement.

The state trooper walked toward her from his squad car. He said all the things he needed to say. Everyone always does. "Did you know you were doing eighty?" he asked. "Got a driver's license?"

When she didn't have the license, he asked her to step out of the car. She did, and when she angled her legs out and straightened, an inch taller than he was, he blinked for a second.

"Sally Condition," she heard herself saying, answering his next question. She knew there would be a million questions, each one knotted to the next. She hated questions. Questions weighed her down. They always had.

They walked to the squad car where she sat in the backseat behind the crisscrossed mesh of screen. She wanted to slip through those lines, but they were made of metal and welded together. A steel net. The trooper talked into his static-laced radio for a minute, then turned toward her. "Looks like we got ourselves a problem, Missy," he said, shaking his head admonishingly.

*   *   *

They cry, and they sob, and they scream at her, and Molly can barely hear their voices. As she sits, hands clasped on the sofa, they beg her to tell them why she ran away. How could she possibly have left all this? Why had she done it?

Their voices soften, and they press for a reason. Her mother's eyes look bloodshot; her face flushes Revlon red. Her father stands in front of Molly, but not too close; he stands, hands on his hips, like he's waiting to get the basketball for a free throw with the game tied, the time clock expired. Molly can hear that expired clock, ticking, ticking. Their voices circle her, tighten around her. "We love you, Molly. We were worried," they say, then in the next sentence they chide her. "How could you do this to us?"

Molly wants to blurt out that she ran away because the road seemed so straight and the tires were so round, because she packed a faded purple backpack, because of the Calvin Klein girl and the basketball. But most of all, she wants to tell them she left because she was too big. That was it, yes, that was it—because she was too tall, and too *big*. She wants to scream it as loud as she can.

Instead, as they lean toward her, demanding an answer, Molly simply says what she's always said to them. And maybe, after all, it was the only answer she can give, the only answer that, deep down, they really wanted to hear: "I don't know," she says. "I really don't know," and she watches them stare curiously into her face as though they're looking into a mirror.

62

SKIP REMEMBERS
The Handkerchief

■ ■ The fragrant scent of cigars wafted through the air when my dad and I sat at the stock-car races at the fairground every summer weekend. I remember the rows of paunchy men, their white shirts untucked, who sat smoking Swisher Sweets and betting on the cars. Then there was the taste of the ice-cream bars Dad bought me as we sat in those the huge, whitewashed wooden grandstands that gave you splinters in your thighs.

Clouds of dust always rose from the dirt track during the races, and when the clouds carried into the stands, it would make me sneeze. Dad would pull a clean handkerchief out of his back pocket, fold it into a triangle, cover my mouth and nose with it, and then gently tie it behind my head like a western bandit's mask. It always made things a little better with the dust and exhaust, and, luckily, I could still smell the pungent, sweet cigars through the linen cloth.

"I always wanted to be a race-car driver," Dad told me once.

"You did?" I responded incredulously.

"Yeah. I wanted to give it a try. I'm getting a little tired of driving town to town on sales trips."

He told me he'd start in the jalopy stock-car circuit, like these races, then work his way up to the sleeker cars and the faster races.

"It's a gamble, but maybe you'd make it to Daytona," he told me, though I was too young to know what that was. "Or who knows, even the Indianapolis 500."

He envied the drivers' skill, their reckless speed, their quick turns and split-second reflexes. He liked it that they could push the accelerator to the floor and keep it there, something he never dared do during his years of salesman trips to the small towns.

I imagined him behind the wheel of a dented car with welded steel pipes along the inside of the roof. A car with no backseats, no speedometer or gauges, and no windows. "The glass would get you in the face," he told me once. You had to go into those cars feet first through the windows, because the doors had no handles and were welded shut. I could picture him—bits of mud plastered to the visor of his racing helmet. He'd wear red leather gloves and white, pinstriped coveralls with Valvoline patches on the arms. I'd see him veering perfectly, swaying between the rear-end collisions, the spinouts that seemed to bring the crowd to its feet at every curve.

At the Cosmos stock-car races, they always kept an ambulance parked just outside the rickety wooden fence that surrounded the track. At least once every night, after a double rollover or a broadside crash or a huge pileup, they needed to rush some driver to the local hospital. Once, a car even flipped and jumped the wooden fence, scattering a few onlookers.

The pileups were always the most exciting part of the races, Dad told me, as long as no one got hurt. I always remembered one spectacular crash in particular—at the far turn, an old bronze-colored Ford with the number 00 went into a skid, slammed the fence, and then stalled sideways on the track. Another car, rounding the turn at full speed, hit the Ford broadside and it did two complete rotations in the air before landing upside down. They had to stop the race for that one—the heavy-set announcer stood at the edge of the track and held out a caution yellow flag, shaking it so all the drivers could see. That time, two men quickly pulled open the wobbly wooden gate for the ambulance.

After the races, we'd sometimes go down inside the track and look at the steaming, splattered beasts that were parked there, their engines still ticking as they cooled. Dad once lifted me through a window and let me sit in a stock car for a few seconds. I was only four or five, and it scared me to see the rusted iron roll bars and the stripped interior that was spray-painted a stark black, so I squirmed out of the car right away. I remember hearing Dad ask a driver if he'd take us for a ride someday after the races.

*   *   *

As we idled at a stoplight on our way home from the track, Dad asked, "Would you like to see me race out there?"

"Sure," I said tentatively, though I was a little nervous about the idea. "But I don't want you to get killed."

"I wouldn't," he chuckled, "I wouldn't."

What was it that I saw in his eyes at that moment as he stared through the windshield? It was something I had never seen before, something I had never known in my father. It was as if he was seeing far beyond the curved glass of the Rambler's windshield, far beyond the one stoplight in the center of Cosmos.

*   *   *

At the start of each race, the sound those stock cars made was incredible. As the cars—twenty or twenty-four of them—would round the north turn in the preliminary lap, they'd backfire, popping like gunshots until that moment when a man, standing right in the middle of the track between the two rows of cars, waved the starting flag. Then the cars sent out a frightening roar as they passed the grandstand; the sound would be so loud I could feel it deep in my chest even though I plugged my ears. Dad and I would stand up, like the rest of the crowd, and shout as the race began.

Once a car spun out and rolled right onto the judge's platform, a large wooden stage in front of the grandstand. The announcer with the microphone had to dash to safety on the grass infield. When he came back, he couldn't locate the checkered flag to wave for the winner, who would be coming around in a few laps. He searched all over the stage, and even under it. He finally found the set of flags—they were pinned beneath the upside-down car on the platform. He picked up the flags and waved them at us, and the entire grandstand burst into laughter and cheers.

* * *

One night, the special feature at the races was an audience participation race; members of the audience could race in some beat-up jalopies that were sponsored by area merchants. The announcer called for drivers from the stands, and a few high-school boys, high on beer they'd smuggled into the stands in paper cups, jumped up. A young mechanic from Cashman's Garage stood up and jogged down the wooden stairway, where the whitewashed paint, I noticed, was worn to gray.

"We got eleven brave drivers up here," the announcer bellowed, hitching up his saggy brown pants. "Last chance for a twelfth."

My father shifted his weight on the wooden boards.

"I should go up there," he mumbled.

"What?" I asked, not sure I was hearing him right.

"I should go up there," he said, a little louder.

I just stared at him as he leaned forward, as if deciding, biting the side of his lip with his front teeth.

Then, all of a sudden, he stood up. He didn't move any further, just gazed out toward the track, the ruts on the straightaway, the weeds, like pieces of scrap metal, spiking along its edges.

"Dad?" I whispered, turning my pleading face toward him.

But he didn't look down at me. I reached for his hand. He squeezed my little hand for a second, almost hurting it, and then let it go. At that moment, all the smells and sounds stopped. All I knew was that my dad was standing there, looking out at the track where a battered car waited for him.

"Dad," I repeated. I could see a wood splinter in the thumb of his right hand.

"Dad," I said again, louder.

Finally he turned toward me, his face red, and smiled weakly.

66

He reached into his back pocket, pulled out his yellowed handkerchief, then shook it lightly in the breeze.

"Here," he said, exhaling a great sigh of air. "We forgot about this. That dust must be really getting to you by now."

He leaned over, and with fingers that seemed to be trembling, tied the handkerchief gently around my face.

SKIP REMEMBERS

Freddie and the Dreamers

■ ■ We knew nothing of explosives. But sometimes, at the end of lunch hour, we'd wake from our naps and remember that we were sleeping inside a bunker that stored 100,000 pounds of gunpowder. We'd wake—while those fleeting dreams we never recalled evaporated quickly from our heads—and squint at the sunlight that always hurt our eyes as it brightened the open front doorway of the bunker. Then we'd lift ourselves slowly from the tar-paper floor, which was coated with a layer of rubber so there wouldn't be any sparks.

At the powder plant, even a tiny spark sometimes meant death. But we never thought too much about that—the plant, three miles outside Cosmos, was just a place to work for the summer, nothing more. It was just a place where, while shoveling gravel along the network of tram tracks, Freddie Crawley and I lifted our shovels to our hips and strummed them like guitars, rocking and laughing as we imitated Herman's Hermits or Freddie and the Dreamers. It didn't matter that we slaughtered the harmonies. We'd dance far up the narrow-gauge railroad tracks playing "Do the Freddie" until Luke, our foreman with the crew cut and bulging, sweat-greased muscles, would look up from his track-straightening crowbar and shout at us to knock it off. As I worked with him, I realized that Crawley knew more trivia about Top 40 songs than anyone in history. The music was simple, maybe even stupid, but we liked it anyway; it helped us pass the time during the tedious hours of shoveling gravel into the hollows between the creosote-soaked wooden ties.

Each day at 11:05, when the whistle blew, we sat on the porches of the storage bunkers and opened our metal lunch boxes. We'd finish our bologna or peanut-butter sandwiches as fast as we could so we'd have a few extra minutes to take a nap. Once in a while, as a gag, Crawley would click his lunch-box fastener back and forth with his index finger.

"Sparks," he'd hiss. "Hey guys, I'm making sparks."

We'd all chuckle nervously, then lie back, resting our heads on the cushioned floor, and let our minds slowly sift down toward the layers of sleep.

All summer long we slept in the powder-storage bunkers not because we were daredevils, not because we wanted to tempt fate, but for simple reasons. We slept there because on those hot, humid days of summer, the bunkers were cool and moist and dark inside. We slept there because they were quiet places, insulated by three-foot thick walls of wood and sod. The first time we stepped into a powder house, I tried not to stare at the red letters painted on the white sign above the doorway: **Danger, 50,000 lbs. of Explosives**. "I'm not going in there," Crawley said, hesitating in the doorway. "No way are you going to get me in there." But we all got used to it. For one thing, you could never see any of the explosives inside—there was just a hollow room with a plain, black floor. The powder must have been stored beneath the floor, or behind the wood and tar-paper walls. The powder houses always smelled like a freshly tarred

69

road, only not as sweet. Sometimes, late in the afternoon, we could still smell that heavy scent on our clothes and skin.

After our naps we woke refreshed; we never had any nightmares. In fact, none of us could quite remember any of our dreams. Crawley once said that sleeping in these damn bunkers was like being hypnotized—when you woke from the trance, you didn't remember a thing.

*   *   *

There were six of us high-school juniors on the tram-track maintenance crew: besides Crawley and I, there was Jimmy Moe, the kid who always tried to talk with a radio announcer's voice; Darrin, the tall, rangy, aloof guy who didn't say much; and Bernard and Ralph, two shy farm boys who decided to forsake their farm labor and come to the plant to make some extra cash. After a few of our musical jam sessions with the shovels, Moe started calling us Freddie and the Dreamers, and the name stuck. We were all kept in line by Luke, our foreman—Luke the Slavedriver, Crawley called him. "You young bastards have all gone soft," Luke used to sneer as he'd stalk down the tracks to make sure we were working. Luke was about forty, and had worked at the plant since it reopened to supply gunpowder for Vietnam; he was even a veteran of the time when the plant operated during the Korean War. "A lifer," Crawley once scoffed. "A regular Zombie," he said, playing off the name of the British rock group. "Probably dreams about this damn place all night."

None of us could come up with a reason why anyone would want to spend their lives working in a prison like this when there was a whole world out there: there was the town square where we circled the Civil War statue, revving the engines of our battered Plymouth Valiants and dented Dodges. There was the rec center where we played ping pong, there was Kunzleman's Soda Fountain where everyone hung out on weekends, where the girls swung peachy legs back and forth from red vinyl stools. The world was the bright green football field beneath the floodlights on Friday nights in fall; the world was bursts of confetti rising from the grandstands, lifted by gusts of wind. It was the weekly Cosmo-Teen dance in the dark school lunchroom beneath the endless sky of purple and pink crepe paper. The world was ours, we thought—we held it in the palms of our hands as we massaged our girlfriends' cashmere shoulders.

At the plant, Luke never slept during lunch break; he usually sat outside on the porch and talked with the older men on the crew. One day when I wasn't tired enough for a nap, I stepped onto the wooden porch and sat next to Luke. As he sipped cooling black coffee from the red plastic lid of his thermos, as he often did, I tried to make small talk with him about the chances of rain and the local ball teams, but he just pinched his small mouth shut and ignored me. For the next few minutes, we had nothing to say to each other; he just sat in his black short-sleeved T-shirt, a blue dragon surrounding the words *2nd Battalion* tattooed on his arm, and stared out at the stretches of gray tram rails that crisscrossed throughout the five–square-mile plant.

Sometimes I think Luke hated us for no other reason than because we were young. When lunch hour was over at noon, he sent me in to wake the rest of the crew. Standing in the doorway, I paused and stared at the guys: they were all lying in a row on their backs with their arms folded on their chests, their mouths gone slack. For an instant, I thought of a line of corpses. Luke walked up behind me and peered over my shoulder.

"Lazy sons of bitches," he hissed through his teeth.

"Not lazy," I said, defending my friends. "They're just asleep."

71

*   *   *

I remember when the news of the plant reopening hit our town a couple of years before. Harley Schuckle, the newspaper editor, came rushing into the barber shop where I sat in the barber chair, white sheet pulled up to my neck. Excited, he gasped about the new government contract, showed us tomorrow's headline, which he'd just written with a pencil on a piece of scratch paper: *Powder Plant Reopens, Will Hire 500.* At that moment, Ned the barber, leaning forward, nicked the back of my head, my perfect crew cut.

*   *   *

Freddie and the Dreamers

As the summer wore on, more and more men from Cosmos quit their low-paying jobs on the city crew or the Park and Rec Department and hired on at the plant for more money. We'd see familiar faces among the men in charcoal gray coveralls. In Vietnam, the war was escalating, and the plant supplied more and more powder for bombs and bullets. Our anemic little town suddenly revived—gunpowder was the new blood flowing through its arteries.

Some of the guys from our crew would eventually get drafted, but we didn't know that then. We just worked the gravel mindlessly—swinging our shovels like pendulums, clanking them into the piles of stones. The guys on the crew didn't talk about Vietnam. The things we talked about most were how the kids at the Friday night dance were doing dances like the pony or the Freddie, or how you could get a good deal on hubcaps at Cashman's Garage, or which song would be the next number-one hit on KDWB radio. Every once in a while, as a stunt, we'd launch into our synchronized footwork, swing our shovels side to side like guitars, and sing "Louie, Louie" in our off-key voices while Moe perched his safety helmet on a post and played drums on it. We never thought about the drum rolls of machine guns in the jungle or the moaning songs of dying soldiers or the last unlucky dance steps of those about to lower their boot onto a hidden land mine. We thought about "Blue Velvet" oozing from the car radio as we slid our arms around our girlfriends and pulled them toward us for that deep kiss that would almost make us explode.

72

*　*　*

After work, while I ate dinner at home, I sometimes watched the evening news on TV with my dad. One night there was a feature on the B-52s; they filmed an aerial view from a bomb-bay door. As the bombs dropped from the plane, they followed each other in a line, wiggling as they fell like tadpoles going deeper beneath the surface of a pond. The bombs hit the ground with a white puff, like silt. Then you could see whitish concentric circles rush out from the center of the impact. It puzzled me, the way those circles expanded across the land. Were those sound waves, or smoke, or what? I wondered. I asked my dad, who was in World War II, but he wasn't sure either. The next news story showed soldiers trudging through a Vietnamese rice paddy, and then it flashed to coffins being unloaded from the open doors of planes somewhere in California. Before the feature was finished, Dad leaned over and switched the channel.

*   *   *

We survived working at the plant only because we liked each other's company, and we were thankful that we weren't working in the powder production lines. We weren't watching the gunpowder come off the conveyor belts, weren't sifting it or loading it into the small rubber-coated tram cars and pushing them by hand toward the railroad tracks, where they were loaded into small bins and towed to a storage bunker to wait for shipment. We didn't want to have to think about where that powder might be shipped, or the bullets it might be packed into. We were glad we worked the railroad crew, where we could drift up the tracks out of Luke's sight and maybe play a few rounds of Name That Tune. The people who worked the gunpowder always walked toward the gate at punch-out time with gray smudges on their hands and face, gray stains on their dark coveralls. Though most of them were from Cosmos, you could hardly recognize them. Some who wore safety goggles all day had gray faces with white circles around their eyes where the goggles protected them. We made fun of them and laughed: "Goddamn racoons," Crawley quipped.

We all agreed that working with the gunpowder was too dangerous. Everywhere you looked in the plant, red and yellow signs were plastered on posts and walls, warning: **Caution, No Smoking Materials Allowed in Plant.** We had all heard the story of the three men who were killed in an explosion the year before we were hired. We were reminded of the incident now and then by Luke and some of the other lifers. The three men were working on the third floor of the chemical building, and everyone said they were blown right through the concrete wall. We tried not to think about those things, unless someone brought them up. Once in a while I thought about the explosion, the circles moving out from it. Sometimes Crawley, gnawing on his lunchmeat sandwich, would turn to us and say "Anybody forget we're sitting on enough powder to launch us into orbit?" We'd all chuckle.

73

Once when I was shoveling gravel with the crew, one of the tram cars, loaded with powder, caught fire. A brilliant red ball of fire rose from the rear tram car. The other guys dropped their shovels, turned and ran across the field. When I saw the cars rolling toward me down the track, I didn't know whether to call out or dive for the ditch, so I just stood there, petrified, unable to move or make a sound. I remember the driver of the tram bailing out into the bushes when he spotted the fire. Luckily, the fire quickly burned itself out without sending a spark to the next car. But I had a dream that night of the one car sending a spark to the car ahead of it, and then the next, until the fire escalated and all twelve of the tram cars were blazing and speeding down the track right toward me. The last car exploded—but in the dream, as in real life, I could not move. I could not move.

* * *

The closest we got to the gunpowder was when, at the end of each day, our crew took a tram along the powder lines to pick up the imperfect or spilled gunpowder and take it to an area called the Burning Grounds. There, at the far corner of the plant, the powder was piled in the middle of a dirt parking lot the size of a football field. At 4:00 each day, a worker who always had booze on his breath slid on his white safety suit and hood with a clear plastic rectangle for his eyes, then pressed the button to ignite the fire. From behind the safety glass in the lookout tower, we'd watch the pile blaze into an orange ball that sent up a mushroom cloud. It was like a bomb going off, but there was no explosion—only a soft, distant sound like a sigh.

The huge gray mushroom cloud rose high, hovered there for a few seconds, absorbing its stem. Then the breeze caught it, and all of us stood there in silence, watching the cloud float into the distance toward town.

* * *

Of our group, some of us eventually got drafted. The next summer, after graduation, Crawley, who never had the money or the grades

Small Dances to an Unheard Song

for college, got nabbed by the Army and was sent to Vietnam. We heard he was a foot soldier over there. The Defense Department had started the draft lottery, where birth dates, written in red on ping pong balls, rolled out of a transparent barrel; if your birth date bounced out first, you were the first to go.

Moe made the mistake of taking a job at the local radio station instead of going on to college, and he was drafted in the fall. I not only made it into college but I was awarded a lucky ping-pong ball: a high number in the lottery.

*   *   *

One afternoon a year later, when I came home for semester break, I picked up the local newspaper and when I read the story, I couldn't move, though my hands seemed to be shaking until the print blurred. Freddie Crawley had been killed in Vietnam.

*   *   *

That summer, we worked at the plant because we needed some spending money. We tried not to think about a war going on. That summer, "I Fought the Law and the Law Won" hit number one; the Thunderbird was our favorite car; and, by late August, though the popularity of Freddie and the Dreamers was beginning to wane, lots of our classmates were still trying to dance the Freddie at the Cosmo-Teen dances. Those noon hours at the powder plant, after we bolted down our sandwiches, we'd crawl back into the storage bunker, stuff our stained cotton work gloves under our heads, and pull our gray safety helmets down over our eyes. Luke would peer in at us and shake his head. "Lazy kids. Damn lazy kids," he'd mutter to himself.

But he didn't understand; we just needed to close our eyes for a few minutes, we just needed to sleep. We'd lie down in our row, hands folded on our chests. After a few minutes, which never seemed long enough, we'd wake. And the strange thing was, though we were certain we had dreamt something, we couldn't remember a thing. Maybe we did dream of bombs or of our fingers playing nervously across the stocks of rifles, but we weren't sure. All we knew

75

was that we'd sleep, and then we'd wake, our minds rising slowly from unconsciousness, our bodies rising numbly from the darkness of the quiet, black floor. Then, the smell of the tar-paper still clinging to our skin, we'd squint and march slowly toward the shafts of bright yellow light that always seemed to be waiting for us, slanting through the open doorway.

PART TWO

AT THE INTERSECTION
OF DREAMS AND ASPHALT

JUNE

The Last of the Rain

■ ■ Wally drives up Water Street into the low sun at eight a.m. in his '52 Buick, and from her garden, June is the only one who watches him leave; the other neighbor women are busy hanging out pure white linens on the wash lines. She thinks she hears the fear, like a distant noise, beginning again. But the man must have a job, she thinks, the same way the white shirts on the wire must have the wind to fill them, to balloon them out until they are dry.

Now she moves from room to room, opening windows. The dry drafts sigh at her from all sides. Yes, the children are her very own. *This is what we must do* she thinks as she looks out at the garden where she spends hours weeding each day, *the wife must do the best she can with the house and the three boys.* But there were some times lately she just didn't know. Today she begins to feel as if half of her mind is being softly pushed out her ears by the breeze, her thoughts seeping into the air like loose strings of clouds. If one of the children got sick or cut a knee, she couldn't decide what to do—she was afraid she'd lose sight of the other two. And the baby always has his mouth slightly open—once a fly flew in, then back out, just like that.

In a few days he will be back, she thinks, back from the roads and the selling of washing machines to businessmen, back from his circuit on the dusty county roads. For a moment she remembers that one time Wally returned after two weeks and acted as if he hardly knew his own children, the way he closed and locked the study door.

She listens to the radio. In a few days he'll call from Sioux Falls or Cedar Rapids or wherever he is and tell her exactly when he'll be home, and she'll tell him about the baby being sick again and ask him what she should do. "He'll be fine in a day or so," he will answer. The Iowa dust will rise from the fields and twine around the telephone lines as they talk, their voices spurting back and forth between distant plastic. *The distance is not really that far,* she'll think.

When she hangs up she'll remember the time she said: "Don't ever leave again," even though she knew all along that he must be behind the steering wheel the next morning and all the way to Storm Lake by nightfall. "All right, I'll see what I can do," Wally had answered as he reached for the hat rack, then slipped off his charcoal coat and handed it to her.

That night, as June read the *Ladies' Home Journal* in her bed it was as though the house was full again. It was as though the bushel basket brimmed with shining red tomatoes. And she reached for the light—"her lamp" he had called it once. Her lamp ever since they began sleeping separately two years ago. But this time when she turned it off, she felt as though she was glowing in the dark—her whole skin a faint silvery-yellow, like a luminous cloud. She wondered if he could almost see her from his room, through the wood slats and the plaster, as if he were awake and not breathing so regularly, a wheeze in and out like the sound of the deep gusts of wind filling the laundry on the line.

At the Intersection of Dreams and Asphalt

He could not have understood her fear. Whenever he left, the fear was a kind of noise somewhere inside her; it started as the hum of a thin metal wire pulled too tightly. It rattled the bed, the whole room, and sometimes spread to the kitchen and even knocked the water glass off the table—the glass she had swept from the tile floor onto the dustpan and not mentioned. It even played and echoed faintly in her head as she fell asleep, like a train whistle that stretches thin but never quite disappears into the darkness of the flat lands.

That next morning it was newspapers; the hush of the sports page in his hands, the headlines of *The Cosmos Freedom* stamped in thick ink, the corner of the advertisement page soaking up brown coffee as if it were dying of thirst. And the two oldest boys fighting and sucking on orange slices, the baby spilling and sloshing tomato juice all over her high-chair tray. This was the way the morning began to inflate after he left: larger, larger, until it floated, a balloon bobbing tautly against the rough plaster ceiling.

*   *   *

But all that was weeks ago, and this morning June is trying to make things different. The oldest has his grapefruit section caught down his shirt and the baby has her fingers stuck inside the milk glass until they're blue, and the middle one has dropped his jelly spoon and is watching it fall the amazing distance from the table-cloth to the floor. June turns her chair toward the window and begins to imagine fleecy-white clouds in the sky—any clouds will do—beyond the thick fading draperies. She hears their mouths behind her with their dark red cries and she waits. She waits.

This is the way all life must be. There would be no life without all this, she thinks as she washes the clothes, hangs them out and lets them dry, then takes them back to the basement and washes them again in her Maytag. Before it breaks down or wears out she has to use it, to make it work for her over and over. The children trace pictures in the dirt of the backyard with sticks from the oak tree and run in circles faster and faster. Then the baby falls and cries louder than the blood on her elbow until June's legs come gasping through long weeds toward her.

By three in the afternoon, June just sits on a blanket in the grass of the yard, staring at the blue, blue sky above the garden, wondering if he will return tonight. She notices the crows that land on the wires each afternoon and stay there until six o'clock or seven, crows that will stick to the dusk like pieces of flat, black paper.

Later, when the children are asleep, she still feels it. It feels like the time Wally rented the flat for a month in nearby Dodgeville, only worse. *The fear, the wire, the noise.* This time it's as though he'll never return, not ever. The noise is making so much racket now in her head that it's the air-raid siren on top of city hall; it's dissolving her brains into something white, something lighter than air. She walks slowly across the hall with the lights out and wants to tell the children she is sorry there will be a hollow spot inside each of them, like the wind-filled arm of a shirt. She wants to flip on the light and tell them *Daddy is gone forever*, but something strong as a clothes-line wraps her fingers into a fist.

She hears the front door click.

He steps into the hallway and stands there, half in blackness, half in the glow of lamplight, and she floods down the stairway toward him, closer toward him. He is back, back for a while and she knows he will be there, asleep in the darkness of the next room for one more night.

82

ROB AND ROXANNE

What Makes It Go Around

■ ■ When the annuity representative arrives at Rob and Roxanne's door, the only thing Rob can think about is sex. Trevor Wichett, sporting a maroon suit with shiny gold buttons, sets down a black briefcase full of account statements and portfolio directors on the living room table. Rob's mind is already sliding toward warm bedrooms, sheets pulled down, the Rolling Stones kicking out an R & B song on the cassette player. Not a CD player, because Rob doesn't even own a CD, wouldn't know how to cue up a song if he did. Rob's strictly from the old school: vinyl from the '60s and '70s, cassette tapes, and lingerie—nice red or passion pink lingerie floating from his wife Roxanne's body as she emerges from their walk-in closet.

When Trevor snaps open the fasteners of his simulated leather case, Rob thinks: lingerie with no buttons. Strictly slip on, slip off. Just thin spaghetti straps on her shoulders, elastic waist-band on her panties. Trevor pulls out some neat stacks of paper, several glossy booklets with pie-shaped designs and pyramids of boxes on them, a gray calculator, and his own personal black pen, a sleek limousine-black one, which he clicks briskly and holds poised in the air above his notebook.

"Now," Trevor says. His nose is so pointed it seems to hurt his face. "Where were we last time?" Trevor recites this as if nothing at all had happened since the last time he set foot in their house; it's as though the entire world stopped because he wasn't sitting with Rob and Roxanne at the dining room table, setting up annuities for their approaching middle years.

On the living room floor, Rob wants to answer, *that's where we were. Our breath getting faster and faster on the living room floor.*

"We were on the short-term fixed accounts," Trevor says. Rob hates it when people answer their own questions, hates it that, lately, the world seems to be carved into tiny gray and white boxes.

"We were on deductions and stability options," Trevor goes on.

Roxy and I were on the beach, thinks Rob, *blood throbbing in our temples, our thighs pressed against each other. That's where we were.*

"You're right, I think," says Roxanne, edging her chair forward, sliding her thighs beneath the oak table and bumping Rob's knee. Roxanne leans forward on the freshly waxed wood surface, and Rob notices the way her arms, crossed in front of her, make her breasts billow upward. She's trying to be polite to Trevor; she wants to plan for their lives together, for their future, and Rob knows this is good.

He admires her for her brain when it comes to annuities and fi-nancial matters; he loves her cerebral cortex for the way it can pro-cess everything this jerk Trevor spews to them about unit values and tax-deferred funds, security bonds, mid-cap indexes.

Rob can't help it if he got a D-minus in high school algebra. Even that grade, the teacher told Rob later, was a gift. Rob tries his hard-est now to think about asset allocation funds, and all he can think of is one thing: the shape of her as she lies face down on the bed, the gentle smooth curve rolling up and over her backside to the small of her back. His gentle fingertips tracing that curve.

"Here's the distribution curve," says Trevor, smiling with the tiniest mouth on earth. "And I think you have to consider your retirement time-horizon and your personal risk-tolerance."

Rob nods, and thinks about his personal risk-tolerance. Thinks about the time he fondled her a few seconds in the closet in her mother's house when she was supposedly getting out a vacuum cleaner. Thinks about the two of them in the backseat of the '65 Olds Starfire parked at a wayside, scrambling for their clothes as a policeman walked toward the car with his flashlight. Thinks about the time when, under a blanket on a small beach, they slipped their suits down, just yards away from a lifeguard and splashing kids. *Yes*, he thinks, *I'm willing to risk a lot for those moments: embarrassment, humiliation, arrest; it doesn't matter.* He considers, for an instant, sliding his hand toward Roxanne's knee beneath the round oak table.

*   *   *

What is it that these visits by an investment advisor do to him, he wonders? Why does an hour-long talk with this man—who spouts statistics about how much the stock market has jumped—make him crazy? He's known Trevor since their days in Cosmos High School, and they both attended the same college; Trevor took classes in accounting, while Rob dabbled in Art 101 and debated whether or not he was going to be the next Van Gogh. What is it about percents and statistics and annualized rates that makes Rob want to—no, not want to but *actually* glide his hand onto Roxanne's knee?

"Rob," she says, a little surprise in her voice, "I didn't know you were putting so little into the growth fund." She nudges him under the table, gives him a tight smile, and brushes his hand aside. She knows it would be rude to carry on that way in front of Trevor, the Chief Financial Advisor for Fidelity Mutual in the heart of downtown Cosmos, as his calling card says. Roxanne has enough sense about her to know that; and she knows Rob would probably go wild, turn from a forty-five-year-old man into a hormone-raging teenager, if she encouraged him in the least. She knows this is strictly business, and she went out of her way to set up an appointment, even left work early, to get this business done. Trevor's represented their retirement account for the past years, but Rob suspects that his company

85

is ripping them off. But Rob also trusts Roxanne to spot the rip-off, if there is one. Her eyes—large, almond-shaped jewels, and clear, like deep wellsprings—have a knack for seeing the world right down to its core: good, bad, nothing escapes those eyes. Rob knows she can penetrate to the truth; she can see right through the thick walls of any person who's telling a lie.

Trevor straightens his little, slump-shouldered body beneath his petite suit jacket. Rob pictures the mass of figures inside his head, blackening his brain.

"Now, in the event that one of you passes away," Trevor recites, "that person's retirement accounts would freeze, and, of course, there'd be no more income from your job. That's why I think you should increase your deposits."

Suddenly, Rob remembers an article he read in *National Geographic;* it said that in some ancient cultures, baskets of corn were more valuable than gold. Other cultures would trade anything for spices or finely woven cloth. Still others valued the grape, or other fruits and vegetables. The article went on to say that during the Cro-Magnum era, cavemen probably traded for fire.

Back then, we traded for what we really needed, Rob thinks. *The things that mattered. That's what made the world go around. But what about now? We covet green pieces of paper with numbers written on them. How stupid*, he thinks. *How far have we really evolved since the ancient days, when fire, and fire's warmth, was a good, simple, valuable thing?*

86

Rob thinks he knows what it is about these visits that bug the hell out of him. All this talk of timed opportunity fund and principle stability and growth and capital preservation is so vague and abstract that he feels like his brain will burst like an overripe melon. He wants to hold something simple and tangible in his hand, like the smooth side of Roxanne's face as he brushes her hair back. Trevor keeps it vague, and Rob knows what Trevor's really talking about is the future; what he's really doing is talking to two people approaching middle age, about retirement and death, and about whatever is left of you at that time. *And what's left?* thinks Rob. *A pile of flesh in an expensive casket, that's what.* It's all about money. It's the world, turning on a dime, like Trevor always says with his off-center grin.

"A mortality fee is charged for all variable-account investments, you know," states Trevor, pointing to a table with his pen.

That says it all, thinks Rob. *You die, and you pay a fee as you cash in your chips. How crass. How utterly crass, how ridiculous.* So he finally opens his mouth and speaks, interrupting Trevor's sentence.

"Why?" The word bursts from Rob's lips. "Why am I paying a fee for *mortality?*"

Trevor pauses. "It's just the way it's done," he finally says.

You robot, thinks Rob. *You goddamn little robot.* "Well, I'm not paying that fee," he states.

"Rob?" Roxanne interjects, alarmed at Rob's tone. She understands rules, regulations, order in a chaotic world. She's the diplomatic one; she might not like Trevor's sharky ways any more than Rob, but she's gracious enough to hear him out.

"I'm afraid I can't do anything about that fee," continues Trevor, tapping his nimble fingers together. His fingertips are too thin, like a kid's, thinks Rob. His palms are too small to ever catch a football. He slides a printed sheet toward Rob. "You see, the fee is calculated each day and based on the average daily net value of each option."

"Bullshit," Rob returns, and he stands, his kneecaps knocking the underside of the wood, jostling Trevor's stack of brochures so they slide across the table.

"You'll have to leave, Trevor," Rob states calmly.

"What?" Trevor blinks.

"You'll have to leave now, because I want to make love to my wife."

As Rob stares at him, Trevor laughs an annoying, nervous laugh which sounds like an asthmatic person clearing his throat. "Heh heh heh."

Trevor tosses the disheveled stacks of papers and fliers into his briefcase, clicks it shut with a loud *snap,* and retreats to the door. "Maybe another time . . . ," he says, ruffled with irritation.

Roxanne watches Rob in disbelief as he ushers Trevor out.

* * *

Rob hurries to the kitchen, pulls a bottle of wine from the fridge. He doesn't care what brand it is, fancy French stuff or a bottle of

Boone's Farm like he bought back when they were in college. All he knows is that it's wine, the nectar of the gods, and he's pouring two water glasses to the brim. It's a taste just bottled last year; a taste as old as time. He's dimming the light, pressing the *play* button on the dining room stereo, and the Rolling Stones blare through the speakers, Mick Jagger's voice singing: *I just wanna make love to you.* The tape turns in circles; the drumbeat is explosive, primitive, certain.

Before he knows it, Roxanne has slipped out of her sweater and skirt and she's swaying toward him as the music seems to play louder, louder, though Rob is not turning up the volume. Rob loves it that the spirit inside her—that deep, unwavering flame at the center of her being—makes her move lithely, gazelle-like, giving her forty-five-year-old body an aura of thinness.

"You're crazy, Rob Hofsommer," she whispers, "and that's why I married you."

Rob closes his eyes and then, somewhere at the back of his mind, in the recesses of that dark cave, the walls covered with petroglyphs, Rob feels a word, a word like a strong tide rising, a word he searches for but can't quite verbalize. It's a word like *fire*, but not exactly. *Passion* maybe. No—it's more like *soul*, only deeper, more intense.

When he opens his eyelids, he sees Roxanne dancing toward him; he crosses the few million years to their dining room. Their arms slide around each other and their flesh brushes lightly, heat radiating from the friction. He presses his lips to the bare nape of her neck, that curve of skin, smooth and perfect as music itself. He'd trade anything, anything for this.

And at that moment Rob is convinced: the world doesn't turn on a dime, like Trevor says. It doesn't turn on a quarter or a silver dollar or a hundred-dollar gold piece.

He lifts his head, stares a few seconds into Roxanne's eyes.

At that moment, he knows exactly, exactly, what it turns on.

DELORES

The Woman Who Dreamed Elvis

■ ■ She waddles from room to room, looking out the windows in case the next person crossing the street might be him. He's already appeared all over her house: Elvis in the mottled pattern of her shag carpet, Elvis's face in the mashed potatoes she ate for dinner, Elvis swaying in the steam rising from her coffee maker.

Delores has real pictures of him in her Elvis shrine, of course—it's a room she's kept since becoming a charter member of the Elvis Fan Club in the sixties. She's got Elvis statues, Elvis salt and pepper shakers, Elvis flowerpots from which green vines curl and snarl. She's plastered her wall with photos of Elvis, and, beneath one lamp, she's got a life-sized Elvis straining from his velvet background. No matter where he is,

Memphis or Vegas or Hollywood, he's always haloed by a spotlight, his silver collar spiking the sky. No matter where he is, he's always staring across the distance and right into her eyes. His eyes, she's often noticed, are blue as the vinyl on *Moody Blue*, his last album.

Delores isn't sure about a lot of things, but she's sure of one thing in this world—she loves him. She loves him, and she knows that if Elvis saw her, he'd love her, too. He'd love her, even though she's a little overweight, straining the seams of her K-Mart slacks. She's a little out of style, her hair sprayed with Final Net and tacked in a bun, her face a little tracked by creases here and there, but, she thinks, not bad for a woman who's forty-eight. She knows he'd love her, not for how she looks, but for what's inside, the cream filling at the center of a bismarck. She knows he'd nod to her without saying a word, reach out for her hand, and pull her toward his motorcycle, which she's seen at an Auto Museum in Murdo, South Dakota. As she gazed at it, she noticed that the shining chrome bars twisted like Elvis's legs when he belted out a song, and the splash guards were studded with rhinestones like his bell-bottoms.

In her daydreams, she's riding on the back of that black-and-silver 1956 Harley, her arms wrapped tightly around Elvis's sequined waist. She feels free as she glides across the landscape. They ride down Main Street and then out of town, past all the flat, dusty farms, toward the border into South Dakota. She pictures a lean Elvis, wearing gold-framed sunglasses, giving her a smoldering look, tipping his head toward her, about to whisper something. Then Elvis's waist widens, and suddenly he becomes Harold, her paunchy ex-husband, and she's bouncing along with him on his old Harley. Harold turns toward her and gives her a stubbly-faced scowl.

Her daydream ends when Elvis transforms into Harold. Maybe she doesn't want to ride any farther, not with that damn Harold, not on that rust-eaten, used Harley that sometimes sputtered and killed at intersections. Not after what he did—leaving her one day, driving off in his pickup to Deadwood or Billings or wherever he went. The point was, he just drove off, and left her here in Cosmos to battle the dry, gusting winds by herself.

It's been two years since he's been gone, and she's never heard a word from him. Not a single word. He might as well have driven his pickup off a cliff into the Grand Canyon. For the past year, she's taken a few correspondence courses and dreamed about leaving town, maybe going to the city and working in a fancy courthouse somewhere. Harold had left his motorcycle in the shed behind the house. He never let her drive it, even though she knew how—said it was *his* motorcycle. "Women don't drive Harleys," he announced to her when she asked. She thinks about how, in the two years since he left, she's never even gone back there and unlocked the shed to look at it. She knows she should just put an ad in the *Shopper,* sell the damn thing.

That evening, Delores watches an episode of *Unsolved Mysteries.* She doesn't miss a show, and she wonders when they'll feature Elvis. She wonders if they'd ever talk about all the clues. How the body didn't even look like him at the funeral. His own relatives hardly recognized him, and they said his face had sweat on it. Sweat, like it was a wax figure—not a real body. And then the other clues: the misspelling of his middle name on the gravestone, the sightings at a convenience store in Michigan and then all around the country.

*   *   *

When she wakes the next morning, she looks at her calendar and sees that it's the first week of August already. As she stares at the squares below the Norman Rockwell illustration, she suddenly realizes that this is the exact date, two years ago, that Harold disappeared. That morning she had wakened and wandered through the house, and he was gone. Just a small stack of cash wrapped in a hand-scrawled note in pencil with some misspelled words. One week in August, Harold left. Then, a week later, Elvis did. She knows there is no holding still: there's no stopping time, no slamming on the brakes, now that she's reached that great middle.

She tosses the calendar and it lands on the floor, flapping its useless wings. It occurs to her that she hasn't had a real vacation since Harold left. She thinks about driving her old Skylark somewhere for a trip. But where can she go where she'd feel free, feel good about herself again? Not to the Badlands, those acres of hot, scorching rocks. That would be torture. Not to Deadwood or the Black Hills, either. Too many bad memories of Harold, near the end of their marriage, getting drunk and dancing with the casino girls and throwing their money away at the blackjack tables.

Suddenly she has an idea—she could drive to Memphis. She could visit Graceland. She could see the King's house, see his rooms, all classed up with wallpaper and decorations, just the way he had left them. She'll walk down Graceland's hallway that's covered with mirrors so you can see yourself, smaller and smaller, walking into infinity.

Maybe she can pick up some clues from snooping around the mansion, maybe she'll be the one to figure out the mystery of how he faked his death and went undercover. She could be the one to tell the press that he was driven into exile, far away to the land no one else wants. That he's probably hiding out with Lakota ranchers somewhere in the west, living a hand-to-mouth life just like he did as a wild, half-Indian rancher in the movie *Flaming Star*.

*   *   *

She rushes into her bedroom, packs her suitcase, then calls her sister in Rapid City to tell her she'll be gone for a week, maybe two. Dressed in dark jeans and a blue plaid shirt she paid almost full price for, she slides behind the wheel of the Skylark. Before she turns the key in the ignition, she thinks *No*.

She leaves the car and hurries back to the house, grabs the key for the shed from the storage closet. She unlocks the door to the small aluminum shed, and there it is: Harold's motorcycle. It looks smaller than she remembered. The leather saddlebags are flat and stiff, its black paint rusted, its chrome dulled. Spider webs connect handlebar to handlebar, tiny glistening tightropes. She opens the gas tank, sees there's still a yellow pool of gasoline. Harold always prided himself on keeping a full tank. Half of it must have evaporated in the two years, she thinks, but it's still half full. She rolls the heavy weight of the bike around to the front of the house, pulls a few clothes from her suitcase, stuffs them into the saddlebags. When she turns the key, the cycle starts with a chug, sputters, then dies. *Women don't drive Harleys* she hears the gravel voice chiding.

She starts it a second time, and it gasps and stops. She turns the key again and this time something catches in her throat and the engine roars, a cloud of blue exhaust rising around her.

92

She drives down Main, the leaning buildings crowding toward her, their windows boarded like blind eyes, and into the open country, leaving whirlwinds of dust behind her. Who cares if Wally in the Rainbow Café or Ned the barber might look out at her and shake their heads?

At dusk, illuminated by the large yellow moon, the straightaway ahead of her narrows to a point on the horizon. *What do I expect to find when I reach that point?* she questions. *What mystery will I solve?*

Her answer is a roar as she accelerates beneath the thousands of stars shimmering like Bic lighters at a darkened concert. The longer she rides, the newer and newer the Harley seems to become—its chrome begins to shine, its faded black paint glistens. Or, she wonders, is it just the play of light on the bike from the full moon? She tips her head back, the cool wind on her face polishing her skin and making her eyes tear at the same time. She thinks she sees something in a swirling pattern of the Milky Way. It's a face—she's almost sure of it. It's somebody's face, distant and close at the same time. And she's certain the face is smiling at her.

93

STAN

The Man Who Chased Tornadoes

He can't exactly tell you why he started doing it. One day he was a dull, middle-aged weatherman on the local station, standing in front of a camera in his pastel yellow sweater, pointing to stationary fronts on a weather map. After work each day, he was content to watch the townspeople stroll along the park by the river beneath a clear sky. Then, one afternoon on the way home, the sudden wind lifted the left windshield wiper from the glass, let it fall back with a *flap*. At that moment he knew his life was about to change.

Some people in Cosmos might be in love with calm days, park benches, walks on the river trails with the cooing song of a mourning dove in the background. Others might be in love with their lives settling down to the ground like so many leaves, like so much dust after the wind has died.

But he is in love with tornadoes.

He's in love with the roller-coaster rise and fall of wind, this rush toward a storm on a gravel road in his converted Chevy van, the clattering hail on the roof of his life. Something makes him try to get close to the funnels, to the huge, dark mouths as if he were about to kiss them.

Ever since he quit the local station and got hired by the National Weather Service, his job has been to drive the back roads, a camera mounted on the hood of his van, a videotape humming inside its waterproof case. When the sky has pulled a wool blanket across itself, he drives off to scan the farm fields for any sign of a tornado. He hopes to enter the storm headfirst, to face the winds, the fist-sized hail, and the drenching rain so no one else has to, so they can huddle with their families, safe in their dry basements or fruit cellars. It's up to him to live the danger so that, a couple days later, long after people have climbed back up the wavering stairs, they can flip on their television sets and gasp at the footage of the tornado that came so close to tearing their lives to shreds.

His goal, from the beginning, has always been simple. Stan Reynolds wants to be the first person to film inside a tornado. Not just near it, or from across a small lake, but *inside* it. He wants to film those few precious seconds of pure spinning terror, the best close-up footage of a tornado ever taken. It'll be almost like a religious experience, he sometimes muses; it'll be like rising toward heaven.

95

*   *   *

So much of this job is quiet, and he's begun to hate that. The calm days, the azure sky, a ceiling that rises high and unreachable. On those days, families are out picnicking, and men with sport coats and khaki slacks stroll casually in the park along the river. At times, as he watches them from the large window of his office, he scoffs at them for their ordinariness. He knows it's a little crazy to think that way, but sometimes a part of him longs for just a few dark clouds, for a sudden curling gust of wind that lifts the hair from the back of his head. Life's too easy if there's no storm, he thinks.

*   *   *

Today started so predictably: a light northerly wind, a passive sky, high cirrus. Barometer steady at 29.90. Then, around noon, things began to change, and Stan could feel that steady change somewhere beneath his skin. A wind lifted its head from the southwest, the humidity rose, and the barometer dropped so low he thought he could actually *see* it fall, as if someone had put a pinprick hole in the glass tube and the mercury was leaking out.

Now the phone rings, startling the still air of his small paneled office. He pounces and picks it up—it's the weather station headquarters, telling him about the massive front moving into the southern part of the state. *All the conditions are right*, the voice says. As if they needed to tell him.

He runs out to his van parked in the back, checks the camera mounted on the roof. He tugs on the bolts, opens the waterproof box to make sure there's enough videotape, then tosses his portable camcorder onto the front seat, just in case. As he clicks the ignition, he imagines the electrical spark, like tiny lightning, firing up the old van.

*   *   *

By the time he's in the next county, he notices a cloud, graying on its underbelly. The sky's face is bruised and angry. He senses the turbulence, the scrape of a dry air mass against a humid tropical front. He's not like everyone else, strolling in the park as though their legs are filled with Novocain, strolling through their lives like sleepwalkers. He's awake. He's alive. His life speaks to him loudly. As he accelerates on the highway, he can hear his heart speaking to him with its impatient voice: *Right now*, it says. *Right now, right now, right now.*

Driving toward the southern counties, he sees the wind whipping the cornfields, a green ocean gone wild. He notices the layer of scalloped clouds above, the swirls of dust devils crossing the road in front of him, and he thinks back on the footage he's taped. Some of the tornadoes are harmless, never touching the ground, lowering a few hundred yards before they're pulled back into the cloud, gently as a snail pulling its gray tail back into its shell. Other times the funnel is black with dust and debris, it's wide and ruthless as it hugs the ground all the way through a town. He's always amazed by those true stories of the oddities a tornado leaves behind: a jar of pickles lifted from a kitchen counter and placed carefully, without breaking, in a backyard five miles away. A penny, driven through a wooden door and then smashing a ceramic piggy bank on the mantel. A woman picked up by a tornado and then dropped harmlessly in a field, a copy of the novel *Stormy Weather* deposited on the ground right next to her.

When he thinks about the destruction he's taped in the aftermath of storms, he can't help but feel guilty. He has to admit it bothers him to see the cars and trucks tossed like toys from the interstate, people's lifelong homes exploded to shards of glass and wood; those images are slivers that puncture his dreams some nights.

And then there are the victims—once they were lying near a water-filled ditch. He remembers coming upon the aftermath of a tornado and seeing fatalities where the victims had no shoes. He recalls how weak and vulnerable the bodies looked, lying there still fully dressed, but barefoot. Lately he's been wondering: If it was going to take their lives, then why did it bother to take their shoes, too—wasn't death humiliating enough? And what was so important about the shoes that the tornado took them? He can't get himself to videotape the victims, so when he comes to a scene where there are fatalities, he always clicks the camera off.

* * *

By afternoon he's in the southwest corner of the state, and the whole sky bleeds gray, a watercolor painting stained all the way to the paper's edges.

Then he thinks he sees something. One cloud begins to twist around itself, and then it lowers toward the ground. He feels the breath suddenly pulled from his lips. He watches the funnel touch down and sway slowly, taking its time as if deliberating about which farmhouse and silo to pluck from the face of the earth, which one to let go free. As it gets closer, he sees its vicious swirling, and for that one instant he's afraid. It's death's arm, reaching down.

But he has to keep his promise with the sky. He has to find out all there is to know about the tornado. He has to understand it, and to let it understand him if it wants to. He wants to see that deadly spiral

The Man Who Chased Tornadoes

up close, looking right back at him with its deceptively smooth skin, ready to pull him in. If his plan works, then he'll walk away from it, free and untouched. He's got to survive it, to show he's not like everybody else.

*　*　*

He veers his van to the gravely shoulder, starts the camera perched on the hood, grabs the portable video from the seat, and rushes to the edge of the field, moving quickly for a big man. There, he stands a hundred yards from a tall, frantic tree.

As the funnel glides toward him from across the field, thoughts snap and spark in his brain: *This is it! I'll be the only person to film inside a swirling tornado and survive. Oz, here I come!*

He stands, bracing himself, gripping the camera tightly, pointing it right at the approaching funnel. He closes his eyes against the stinging dust but holds the camera steady.

My God, the roar! He can't begin to explain the roar in his ears. It's not like a freight train, like they always say—it's a million voices, high and low, screaming all at once. A million voices, some living, some dead, and some in between. Then he feels the burning pain, as if the wind is trying to peel all the skin from his body.

*　*　*

When he wakes, a gentle rain is falling. No wind on his face, just the gentle rain tapping his cheeks, his closed eyelids. He's not sure where he is, if he's in heaven or the bright land of Oz.

He slowly opens his eyes, blinks the rainwater away.

Gray above him. No color or shape, just solid, moving gray. He lifts his head and looks around. He's still in the flat field, though he's not where he was when the tornado approached. He sees the splinters of the single tree at least two hundred yards away. Then he sees his dented van, flipped upside down in the ditch by the road, the camera and tripod crushed beneath it.

The silence is broken by the haunting sound of the faraway sirens, and he says a quick prayer. He hopes no one's been hurt by this tornado. There's a price to pay for everything, and he hopes it's not that.

*　*　*

Then he spots his video camera, a few feet from him. It's lying sideways in a shallow pool of water. The camera's waterproof, of course, so he doesn't worry. His whole body aches as he reaches toward it. The red light is on, which means the camera is still recording. It's pointing right at him. Him, Stan Reynolds, the sacrifice, the survivor. Though his brain aches, the headlines rush through his head: *Amazing Footage: Storm Chaser Videotapes Inside A Tornado and Lives*. For an instant, he imagines a Weather Channel special, selling the tape every meteorologist would die to watch.

But when he turns the camera over, he gasps: the tape cartridge is open, and the cassette is gone. It's been sucked out of the camera by the cruel funnel, swallowed into the belly of that spinning gray whale. He looks into the viewfinder and it's blank, like the inner lining of the brain after it's just forgotten a dream.

Then, for an absurd few seconds, he pictures the plastic cartridge, still high inside the funnel, still rotating around and around with the trees and lawn chairs and bicycles. He pictures the gray tape itself, being pulled out of the cartridge, the plastic ribbon being wound around itself as it spins, a miniature plastic twister within the twister.

He looks up and curses the sky, a sky that's still menacing and impenetrable. And then he curses himself for wanting to chase storms in the first place. He glances down to see that he's lying there barefoot, his feet—pale and bluish—sticking out from the cuffs of his trousers.

99

He begins to sob, not for the tape that's gone, not for the footage he's lost. He's sobbing because he's just a human being, without shoes, and nothing more. He's sobbing because something tells him that, before too long, he'll be one of those people by the river. He'll be strolling there on a sunny day, barefoot by the river in the park. And when one small dark cloud appears he'll look up and scowl at it a few seconds and then, as though he'd never noticed it, he'll turn his head the other direction, where all he can see is the vast blue sky.

RUSSELL AND KERRI

Train Whistles, Flights of Geese

Sometimes, to her, he is the sound of a distant train whistle. To him, she is the silence between each whistle.

Lately, she tells Russell his face has been taking on a look of distance, tells him he seems too far away. *Maybe I am,* he thinks. Maybe he's in another part of the country, riding in some dim boxcar, his pupils widening as much as they can just to see the landscape slide by outside. And maybe lately she's taking on that look, too. This morning she told him that, unless he agrees to move, she's leaving him.

* * *

Russell used to like to walk the tracks in the early morning. To see the freight cars loaded with gravel, to startle the pigeons that lifted by the dozens into the dawn sky as they flew over the rails. Those moments, the sky seemed to be all shimmering, all wings. Those moments, he thought how unbendable the rails are, yet above them, there was all that motion and pattern.

He remembers the heat wavering above the rows of tracks in the hot August sun. The shade beside the loading car was always cooler, and he'd sit on the gravel and eat his lunch there with his work crew. Sometimes he'd reach up with a pointed, chalky piece of gravel and scratch his name into the side of the freight car.

He knows he's been thinking too much lately of the early days, when he had that first job loading crushed gravel into the railroad cars.

* * *

A few weeks ago, Kerri started talking to him about moving. She frequently mentioned moving, but this was different—he sensed an urgency in her voice. She was tired of this place, she said, tired of making the best of it. She said the only thing she liked about living in Cosmos was that the geese were always migrating over it in fall and spring. She loves to watch the geese gliding high in the air, like stitches on a patchwork of blue and white. Loves how, sometimes, they fly silently in a single row. Last week she bought wooden goose decoys at a garage sale, then stuck them in the crabgrass of their narrow front lawn. Geese heading south on the flyway and crossing on their way down from the lake country might be lured to rest in the yard, she told Russell.

So far, no geese have stopped.

* * *

In the old days, before he met Kerri, Russell used to sleep in a rooming house above the Cold Spring Tavern, near the quarry and the freight yards. Cosmos was a connecting point for shipments of grain and corn heading west and east. From his window, he could see the tracks—half shining in the early sun, half rusted. He felt the floor of the room shiver whenever a freight trundled past on its way from Fargo to Sioux City.

At first the sound of the freight cars rumbling at night kept him awake. But later he actually began to like it: he'd fall asleep to that rhythmic music coming in through the screen. He began to wonder why other people wanted the sound of a lake shore, or crickets, or a soft radio. All he wanted was the rise and fall of diesel engines, the drumbeat of boxcars coupling and uncoupling, the scrape of steel wheels as they polished the rust from the tracks in the moonlight.

*   *   *

Some nights, at two or three, she sits up in bed. She wakes him and asks, "Did you make that sound?"

"What sound?" he mumbles, coming up from the depths of sleep.

"That sound. Kind of a moan."

"I don't know," he says. "Maybe it was my foot again."

"Does it hurt right now?" she asks.

He rubs his puffy eyes. "I'm too numb to tell. Go back to sleep."

Sometimes at night the foot he broke years ago still aches. He has a hunch he's feeling the pain during his sleep, maybe reliving the accident, and groaning without even knowing it.

*   *   *

Before he was unemployed and the two of them were living off Kerri's waitress job at the Rainbow Café, Russell and his crew used to load five or six railroad cars in one day, the gravel pouring against the metal floor of an empty ballast car, a sound like those steady cymbals that get louder and louder at the end of a symphony.

Russell still remembers when the big steel wheel of the gravel tram caught his left leg. He could feel the bones in his foot collapse like a handful of toothpicks, and he was damn certain that when they pried the cart's wheel off his ankle, his left foot would be wide and flat, like in a cartoon. But when he glanced down through that awful fire of pain, the foot looked the same. Just the same. He almost laughed.

To his way of thinking, it never healed right. He went back to the company doctor a few times, but the bones weren't like before. Like old lovers who broke up, they could never come back together exactly the same. His wife massages his foot now and then. She tells him "It'll heal, it'll heal. Sometimes things like this can take years."

*   *   *

He used to tell her some of the stories about his quarry job, and she listened to them. But after a while she didn't want to hear them anymore. "Same story," she said. "I've heard that one at least half a dozen times." She would straighten her small back and tilt her head, her curled brown hair not moving.

Lately, he's reminiscing too often, she tells him. Then, with one easy turn of her face, she glides miles away from him.

*   *   *

When they can't stand it in the house one more second, Russell drives Kerri out into the country, to the flatlands west of town. Russell doesn't like rolling hills in his landscape; he doesn't like all those trees and brush and confusion. Give me the flat plains, he says, where he can see as far as his eye can throw its sight. West of Cosmos, way out near the South Dakota border, what you might think is an eyelash on your eye turns out to be a radio tower miles down the road. You see things three hundred and sixty degrees, and he feels like you own it, you own it all.

They don't own their house, though. They rent; but it's the best they can do on their income. The house is narrow, wedged between apartments built in the forties. Chipped green siding. Beveled wooden pillars hold up a tin-roofed porch. Inside, a paneled living room, pink-tiled kitchen, a cramped rectangular bedroom. When the lilacs bloom each spring and lean over to their side of the fence, Kerri picks a few and surprises the rooms with their scent. Little purple plumes explode from plastic tumblers, beer bottles, whatever is handy. She's like that, thinks Russell: she can take something plain and somehow turn it sweet.

Kerri's originally from the city. Not a big city, but a city just the same. When he first met her, she didn't look small-town; she looked a little pampered—her shiny blouses, her hair curled just right. She keeps asking to go visit Minneapolis, a couple hours' drive from where they live. She keeps talking about spending weekends there, going to plays or sitting in a restaurant with white tablecloths, roses in a vase, and a view of the skyline. "We'll go," Russell assures her. "We'll go some time."

A few times these past weeks she's stared at him and asked: "What's keeping us here?" He can tell by her tone she's on the verge

103

of cracking. But he can never answer her when she asks that; it's something he never even asks himself. He can't explain it. If he moved, he'd only move west, toward the Dakotas where he grew up as a boy, to that lakeless place, to that place where the landscape flattens as if two people took a rippled sheet and pulled it taut from opposite corners. But he can't tell her all that. So he just shrugs when she asks, and maybe lights his pipe so he has something to gnaw on besides the lack of words.

There are times when he feels she might be right. It might be a good idea to move, he thinks. But he can't pull himself out, not right now. If he moved to a city, he'd feel like one of those plants they grow in a greenhouse without soil, its roots just floating there in the air.

* * *

"Whose name are you calling?" she asked him last night after she shook him awake.

He didn't answer.

"It sounded like someone's name," she said.

"Just a dream," he replied. "Some kind of dream."

But as he lay there, he thought he knew whose name he was calling. He was calling himself—his own name. Calling himself before he broke the foot. He was trying to bring out words to warn himself to move quicker, to jump for it, to leap out of the way of that runaway tram car before the heavy, rusty wheel pins him to the track.

Then, before dawn, he woke and sensed that she wasn't in bed next to him. He looked around and saw her standing at the bedroom window, gazing down at the yard. He climbed out of bed and slid his arms around her waist. It didn't startle her, and she didn't turn toward him.

"Geese," she said.

"Decoys," he said.

"No," she insisted. "I heard them. Geese."

* * *

This morning at breakfast, they argued. She told him that unless he agrees to go somewhere else, to try something besides this shrink-

At the Intersection of Dreams and Asphalt

ing town with no jobs, besides this house where the rooms seem to be getting narrower and narrower until it hurts her to breathe, she's leaving. Finally, after hours of arguing, she stomped into the bedroom and shut the door. He just stood there in the living room, his fingers clawing at the cramping muscle of his left leg. At that moment he felt like the two of them were like the railroad tracks—steel lovers always keeping the same distance apart but afraid to leave.

They didn't talk to each other the rest of the day. She stayed in the bedroom, filling in crossword puzzles, and he strolled downtown, sat in a hard plastic chair and read the paper at the Rexall Drug store. In the afternoon, when he pushed the front door open again, he saw her gathering up her magazines from the kitchen table and, without looking up, retreating into the bedroom.

Now he stands outside the door, his left leg aching. He knows tonight he'll probably fall asleep to some faraway train whistle. He's not sure at such moments whether he's moving toward her or dissolving into some flattened distance. But he thinks he's moving toward her, slowly. Like a dot on the horizon growing larger, he's moving toward her. If he's the train whistle, then she's everything that exists between those whistles; she's the rest of the world, surrounding the whistles with a soft silence.

* * *

Late that night, during the sound of a whistle, they both wake at the same moment. He lies there, hands squeezed into fists. Without saying a word, she lifts herself up, slips toward the end of the bed. He can feel her now, reaching down under the sheets and touching his left foot. Just one finger, at first. Then her whole warm palm caresses it, and he sits up and touches her arm, frail as a bird's wing.

It's then that the pain gets smaller and smaller, slides off into the horizon so he can't imagine ever having felt it. For a moment, all that pain goes away.

NORM AND JOHNNY
The Everyday Drive

I don't know why I go to these races with Johnny. We sit on splintered wooden bleachers and watch the stock cars, the battered beasts circling, kicking up dirt as they roar around the track, swerving occasionally to dodge a dull bumper or a piece of sharp chrome that's just fallen off the car ahead of them. All I know is that it's beautiful out there, just too beautiful.

Johnny and I come to the races to bet on the cars and drink some beer. Maybe the car I picked will come in first, or maybe Johnny's car—the one he put together at Townsedge 66 from parts he got in the Cashman's Auto Dissembling Center—will beat mine out. As the cars whip past the checkered flag, the pop of backfire echoes like something softly exploding inside our chests. After the cheers from the crowd die down, Johnny, leaning back and taking a drag from his Marlboro, one thick eyebrow cocked, will look at me, his grease-stained palm open, and say something like "The world is perfect, my friend. Now where's my ten spot?"

I'll reluctantly pay him the ten bucks and then we'll wait for the next feature—the late model modifieds—and I'll sip a beer and Johnny will finish the Marlboro that he pulled from the pocket of his white shirt with the short sleeves rolled up around his biceps. The red and white label always shows through, just above the spot where his heart is.

The thing is, though we go back a long ways, Johnny and I are really different now that we're pushing thirty-five. Sometimes I don't know why I sit here, halfway up on the sagging bleachers where the mosquitoes start hitting you just after dusk and the clouds of dust rise from the track as the cars thunder away from the green flag. And then there's the pungent scent of burning metal that wafts across the stands every once in a while when a car's engine goes bad, a cloud of blue smoke rising from the tailpipe. There are fragrant scents here, too: cheddar-flavored popcorn and corn dogs and spilled beer, of course, and the taste of Rollos, which I always buy at the concession stand. I know the roar of the cars carries all the way to the new development on the hill on the north side of town, where I live. When I'm at the races, I sometimes imagine people who live in those sprawling brick houses, walking out in the evening to sprinkle their lawns, suddenly looking up with a little fear on their faces and wondering *What's that sound?*

It's no secret why Johnny goes to the races; he's worked on some of these cars at the Townsedge, welding the roll bars, tinkering with the engines. He's been doing that ever since high school, which is far behind us, already almost fifteen years down the track.

Johnny and I have a long history together. Growing up next door to each other, we were two boys in the backyard, hardly talking, playing with our Tonka trucks, scraping them back and forth until they wore tracks in the dirt. We put notes in bottles, tossed them into the flow of the Cosmos River, sending our cryptic messages to someone who might find them downstream: *This note was written by King Johnny and Duke Norm, the year of our Lord 1724. If you find it, please call 332-3221*. In grade school we were altar boys at the seven a.m. Masses at St. Stanislaus, where we yawned and snickered; and then there was the freshman football team, where the two of us—me a second-string wide receiver and Johnny a backup tailback with pretty good speed—rode the bench. Both of us looked for girlfriends as we drove the south shore of the lake in my father's cream and black Ford. At seventeen, we leaned beneath the hoods of cars over that dark, mysterious landscape called the engine, checked the oil and changed the plugs. We talked about horsepower and miles per hour and how fast we could drive past the city limits sign—and with which girl, a tight pink sweater pulled down to show her bare shoulders.

So when Johnny calls me once in a while about going out to the races, I don't even think twice before blurting "Sure." These last years we have something else in common—that big beyond called *adulthood*, called *approaching 35*.

"The thing is," Johnny says to me after the car I picked to win spins out and slides down the muddy bank on the first turn, "you don't know how to pick a car. The thing is, Normy," he adds with a kind of kidding confrontation, "you think you know where you're going, but you don't know jack shit."

Then I counter with, "And you think you do, my friend?"

"I know cars," he says flatly.

"And I know houses."

"I know carburetors. Fuel valves." He ends the conversation with a long drag on his Marlboro, letting the smoke out in a thin, long stream that carries up and over his head. That's when he does his James Dean pose, tipping his head to one side and holding that Marlboro so loosely it looks like it could drop from between his fingers at any second. *I could know a lot more, too,* he's probably thinking, and I'd have to agree with him. Johnny actually did pretty well in high school, and could have gone into a lot of different fields, but he just never had the ambition.

The big difference between the two of us is that I went on to college and ended up a top realtor and housing developer at Midwest Homes. Johnny stayed on at Townsedge 66 after senior year, where, though he never made the basketball team, he dribbled inner tubes from Toyotas and then shot them ten feet into the pile at the back of the concrete-block building, shouting as if he'd just scored the winning basket in the NBA championship. Now I lean over blueprints for new houses, smoothing their curled corners, and Johnny leans over a fender at Cashman's Auto Dissembling Center, a place piled with wrecked cars where engines hang on chains or sit on counters, the grease pooling beneath them.

Once, on the way to my office, I pulled my new Town and Country van in front of Cashman's to say hi to Johnny. No one was around, and I walked into that dim garage. I didn't know why, but for some reason, I felt uneasy, almost afraid of the car parts that surrounded me: the battered doors leaning against the concrete wall, the rows and rows of glass windshields, stacked blind on wood beams, the ghostly pale pile of plastic washer-fluid tanks, the boxes of greasy engine parts rising in gray-black pyramids. In the back corner, the jungle of mufflers and bent tailpipes squirmed like snakes.

What scared me most of all was the half-car sitting just at the edge of the doorway. The red car had no front end—no engine, dash, windshield, or front doors—as if someone had simply cut it in half. The steering wheel rose starkly from the base of the floorboards. Sunlight slanted into the two front bucket seats, and a dusty stick shift with a leather knob angled between them. A glitter of broken glass spewed across the carpeting of the front seat, a green bottle of Mellow Yellow lay sideways, half-empty, beneath the driver's seat, and a few scraps of paper and foil candy wrappers decorated the floor. I cringed as I noticed something reddish, like dirt, or blood, staining the gray floormat. The longer I looked at it, the more I realized this car was not being stripped down by Johnny, but it had been *towed in* this way after an accident—a head-on, no doubt—which tore the front end right off. I pictured the accident, the terrible crunch of metal and glass, occurring during someone's everyday drive. It probably happened right in the middle of what this driver thought was a safe road, maybe while chewing a few Rollos and about to take a sip of Mellow Yellow. That's when you least expect it, I thought, when you're washing down caramel and chocolate with a sweet sip of soda.

That half-car gave me a chill, a quiver I couldn't quite understand, and at that moment I just had to look away from it. I looked away and noticed Johnny's girlie calendar on the wall, the blonde luxuriating on the hood of a Chevy, the large Xs crossing off half the days of July. Then Johnny's silhouette appeared in the doorway, his body lean but kind of coiled as he carried half a White Castle burger in a wrinkled paper wrapper.

"What's the story on this one?" I nodded toward the red car.

"No story," he replied. "Just another speeder." He glanced toward my Town and Country, parked outside the garage door, then quipped, "So, you bringing that thing in for salvage?"

Whenever I stop by Johnny's, which isn't that often, it's those highway wrecks that scare me the most. Johnny has pointed a few out for me, revealing the salient information with just a few simple words in his matter-of-fact voice: "Side-on," he'll say, and leave it at that. Or "head-on," or "rollover." These vehicles are nothing like the stock cars, all the glass removed and replaced by steel mesh or black rubber netting, the doors wired shut so drivers have to climb in through the window. Those cars thump dully into one another around the turns, denting their soft fenders but not budging the steel pipes buried in their frames. It's nothing more than entertainment for the two thousand fans who pack the stands of the Golden Spike Speedway each Sunday wearing cheap black or canary yellow T-shirts sporting the numbers of their favorite drivers. Sure, there are pileups on the south curve, and drivers sometimes get hurt; but they're controlled crashes, and it's the chance the drivers take.

110

"Everything's a calculated risk," Johnny always says, whether he's tearing a bumper off an old Dodge or grabbing a quick Friday afternoon beer with me at the Eagle's Club, a place he actually sneaked into senior year because he looked old enough. "Everything. Your life. My life. But where's it get us in the end?"

Johnny's got a really good point, and as he looks at me with his square jaw and his swept back, slightly receding hair, I have no comeback. I just sit there and shrug and give him a sheepish look that says *You got me. You sure got me, buddy.* I remember that he got an A in our philosophy class junior year; he doesn't say much, but when he says something, it somehow makes too much sense, kind of pushes me off balance. That's what I like, and it's also what makes me uneasy about Johnny.

The point is, I don't know why I hang around with Johnny anymore, his white T-shirt always sagging at the neck in a little smile. At the same time, I can't help but wonder why I feel so different from the men in beige suits and red-and-blue ties who run my company. In my office, I work with paper plans for houses; I sort dry manila folders that stack one upon the other, but I never touch the houses. Someone else brings out the hammer and boards and ladders and builds the houses while I watch from my tinted second-floor office window. I see them going up in the new development on the east side, the two-by-six boards filling in the roofs like ribs.

"What you should get is a real job, working with your hands," Johnny says as we sit at the races, waiting for the next heat. He props his black boots on the bleacher in front of us. "Maybe learn to drive a Ditch Witch or something."

"What you should get," I counter, knowing he can't help but resent my career a little, "is a job where you might use half a brain."

"What you should get," Johnny says, finishing off the conversation with a twisted-lip smile, "is screwed."

* * *

Johnny's been divorced for five years, lives on the south side of town where the rundown houses seem to lean against one another for support in the hot summer sun. I live in Walden Woods with my wife and two kids, with an economy Corolla in the double garage and a minivan out front with Care Bears and Beanie Babies covering the backseat. We have a kiddy pool in the yard and an eight-foot redwood fence around it. Each morning I take the smooth drive to the Midwest Homes & Realty, walk into a plush office, and lean over a large sheet of blank paper spread out on my rosewood desk. Lately, the more days I stare at it, that sheet of paper seems bigger and blanker. Lately, it's beginning to look like a huge map to nowhere.

* * *

"A perfect night," says Johnny, as the cars rise up the dirt ramp from the pit and onto the track for the next short-tracker heat, "is a beer in the hand and a Chevy Nova with a set of Goodyears crossing the finish line." He's referring to his car, sponsored by Townsedge, which

111

just won the last heat and earned him my ten bucks. He's referring to the two-hundred-fifty-dollar GXT100 extra wide tires that he himself personally lug-nutted onto the hubs late Saturday.

*　*　*

After the feature race is over, I hop into Johnny's truck for a ride back to my house. He spins out of the Golden Spike, the bumper swishing through the high grass of the field that doubles as a parking lot. There's a six-pack of Bud on the seat between us, and he pops open a can and then offers me one. The '79 orange Chevy truck's dash is stripped down—all metal—and there's a rectangle where the radio's missing. There's a two-inch hole rusted in the floorboards on the passenger's side, hidden beneath the grimy orange carpet mat. "Ventilation," Johnny explained.

Before we reach the city limits, Johnny takes a quick detour toward the Sherburn Wildlife Refuge, a forest preserve that's crisscrossed with a maze of narrow sand roads. He pulls the truck to a stop on one of the roads, opens another can of beer, stares through the windshield.

"Aren't you dropping me off?" I ask.

He chugs his whole can of Bud in a few seconds. Then he says, "When I was in high school, I came out here in my old man's Buick and drove these roads all night." His dad is Wally Lauder, who, for years, has been the Businessmen's Club president.

"Yeah?"

"I was trying to figure out what to do with my life."

"So what'd you find out?"

He pauses four or five seconds, then, as if to answer, presses the accelerator to the floor, the sand spewing out beneath the back tires. I'm pushed back against the torn upholstery of the front seat. I can tell, by the way it jumps, that Johnny has souped up the engine of this old truck. He speeds down the road, turns quickly left on another smaller road, which is more like two tire ruts between a row of trees. The headlights illuminate the tall, scruffy pines on either side.

"I drove like this," Johnny says, his face intense though still somehow relaxed, his bushy eyebrows closer together on his high forehead. "Took these roads fast." I watch the trees whipping past in a green blur and see the speedometer needle rise near 60. "Fast as I could. Never spun out. Never hit a goddamn tree," he says. "That's what I needed to do in high school. That's the speed I needed to go." He turns his face toward me, and I'm nervous that he's taking his eyes off the road for a couple seconds. "Know what I mean?"

"No," I say, hoping maybe to calm him down. "Not really."

"Come on," Johnny says, gunning it around another corner. The force of the turn shoves my right shoulder against the door and I feel its cool metal. "You *know* what I mean. We've known each other *that* long."

I clutch the armrest as Johnny takes a fast right turn, the old truck leaning on its suspension.

"This too goddamn fast for you?" Johnny asks, shouting above the engine as the speedometer jiggles toward 70. "Does it scare you?"

I can see by his eyes—their narrowed, molten look—that something's eating at him tonight, but I don't know what.

"There might be somebody walking out here," I caution. "I mean, you'd never see them in time."

"So you want me to slow down?" Johnny asks.

"No." I hesitate, then add, "Well, yeah, maybe."

He doesn't slow, just veers the truck down another narrow dirt path. The boughs of the pines whack against the rearview mirror on Johnny's side, scrape against the door panels. The carpet mat has slid sideways, and I think I can see the dirt road rushing beneath the rusted hole in the floorboard. "Your life is always so goddamn safe," he says. "You and your big degree. Your big-time job."

"Let me out," I blurt. "I've had enough." Johnny's drunk, and he's turning hostile. I saw him get this way once at a senior rec-center dance when he got into a fight with the quarterback from the football team.

He keeps driving a few seconds as if he didn't hear me. "Whatever you say," he finally says, his voice flattening out. He hits the brake and the truck slows. When it comes to a stop, I jump out. I still clutch the can of beer in my hand; I can feel the bent aluminum where I squeezed it hard in the middle. I hear Johnny, sniffing a little as he inhales the exhaust fumes through his open window. Hear him crack open another can of Bud, take a long drink.

113

When Johnny guns the truck down the long straight road, his red taillights shrinking, I don't know what I'm going to do next. For the first time in a long time, I have no plans at all. It's like my life has been cut off, right here on this road. It's as if I'm starting my life over, right here.

Maybe I'll walk all the way back to town, I think. It's a few miles, but I figure I could get back to my house by three or four in the morning. Maybe I'll try to hitchhike on County 66; then I wonder— who would pick up a lone hitchhiker at midnight? I consider staying here, under the moon, sleeping beneath a pine tree until morning. But I forgot to bring my cell phone tonight, and my wife and children would worry. There'd be police cruisers out looking for me by dawn. When they find me, eyes bloodshot, wrists scratched, wandering through the thick pines, I'd explain, simply, to the puzzled cop: "Johnny. It's all Johnny's fault."

Or maybe I won't do any of those things. I might just stand here in the middle of a dirt road in the middle of the night and do none of those things. I'm starting to think that life is about doing none of the things you planned; instead, you end up standing on a small dirt road in the middle of nowhere and letting what's left of the moonlight fall on your skin.

And just as those thoughts start riding through my brain, I see a pair of headlights flare, hear the roar—a roar I recognize as a juiced-up, 409 horsepower engine inside a rusted-out '79 Chevy truck body with faded orange paint. Somewhere in Walden Woods, someone who couldn't sleep might be standing in their quiet backyard and looking up suddenly, wondering what in the world that sound is. The yellow headlights aim right at me, jostling up and down a little as the truck bounces on ruts. I can tell Johnny's flooring the truck by the way it accelerates, the blue exhaust smoke rising behind it in the moonlight. He's like some mad stock-car driver, going all out on the straightaway, because you know the turn's coming up soon. There's always a big curve just ahead, where you might spin out and slide to a stop down the steep, muddy embankment.

Johnny drives right at me, and I just freeze there in the middle of the road. As he approaches, I can make out his damn switch blade sneer in the orange glow of the dash lights, his teeth clenched behind those baby-boy lips. At that moment, I believe he's going to cut me in half. Though I'm panicking inside, I cross my arms and brace myself as the truck gets closer and closer.

Then, just as he's within a hundred feet of me, he slams the brake and the truck slides on the dirt, slides right toward me with a sound like a long sigh. The bumper finally comes to a stop just a little ways from my knees, and the engine kills. Though I try not to, I know I flinch a little, and blink at the billowing dust cloud that floats over the truck and surrounds me.

Angry, I shake my head and think *This is it. I'll never talk to that crazy son of a bitch again.* Then, in the silence of the killed engine, I suddenly hear a sound. It's a laugh. It's a high-pitched cackling laugh I recognize, having heard it since I was a boy. It's a laugh I can feel inside my chest, half sane, half insane, and for a moment I want to join in and laugh along with it. Instead, I'm silent. I keep the laugh deep down inside, where it's safe.

I hear a friendly voice mumble, "Get in, buddy."

I don't answer, just stand there, my Doc Martens not moving, and I smell that burning-cinder scent of the overheated engine.

He leans out the window, his white short-sleeve shirt rolled on his bicep. "C'mon," he chuckles. "Get in. I was only trying to scare you. I didn't mean nothing."

I look down at the bumper, inches away, its chrome dulled and corroded. At that moment I know that Johnny and I are this close. *This* close.

Johnny cranks the ignition and the truck starts. It's then that the wind picks up, a pine bough sways in the breeze like it's about to dance, and the world starts turning again. Above me, the moon slides ever so slightly in its orbit across the starlit sky. I feel my feet move. Though I never thought they'd move again, I feel my shoes shuffle, kicking up a little dust.

Before I know it, I'm striding around to the passenger's side of the truck.

"Hey, Johnny," I call casually, like we've been introduced for the first time, and I climb back in.

115

DOMINIC

Falling Away

Nobody in town really knew what it meant, though they talked a lot about what happened that one morning in church. People like Dominic Bodaway, whose wife passed on years ago, seemed to go through the motions in life, painting his small frame house and then, two or three years later, the paint would peel off, so he'd sand it down and paint it again. Night after night he sat at the kitchen table and filled in crossword puzzles—different boxes with the same twenty-six letters. Around ten o'clock, he'd pour a shot of Jack Daniels in a Mount Rushmore souvenir shot glass. Then he'd flip on the light to his wooden back porch. The 60-watt Soft White bulb, not too bright, nor too dim either, would glow until morning—in case there was trouble, he figured, or someone in need, which there never seemed to be.

Then he'd get down on one knee and recite the Our Father that he'd said since grade school—the same fifty-five words, followed by a quick sign of the cross. He rattled through the prayer the way you'd recite your address or phone number—the words were just something your lips had memorized, and that was about it. Dominic practiced his religion; he'd attended a grade school and a high school taught by nuns and, for the past twenty years, he was head usher at St. Stanilaus, a church he'd attended for almost all of his seventy years. He'd held rosaries and plastic statues of the saints, gazed at pictures of Jesus at the back of the church, let the thin host melt on his tongue, and dipped his hand into the marble bowl of holy water coming and going; but he didn't really feel any sudden inspiration, any burning or cooling beneath the skin of his fingertips. It was like his skin was always a little numb, too thick to feel what it was supposed to. And no matter what he did, the world was always out there—its wars, its fighting, its stalled cars and travelers stranded in the night.

After his evening prayer, he crawled onto his saggy Posturepedic to sleep on the right side. Though he had the whole bed, he always slept on the right side. There were always good reasons for things you did, he figured, even if you weren't sure exactly what they were.

It was usually a deep, blank sleep, since Dominic never remembered his dreams, though he was pretty sure he had them. Then he'd wake at seven twenty-one—always seven twenty one, no earlier, no later—to a beeping alarm that sounded like a maintenance truck backing up toward him. For breakfast, it was two eggs over easy, no broken yolks, salt, no pepper, wedge of toast with grape jam, and, in the background, a blaring morning talk show on WKOS, where the townspeople called in to bicker about the Vikings' chances to get to the playoffs, why vandals uprooted the purple cosmos in the flower bed down on the town square, or whether to put a stop sign at Jupiter and Elm—a street still called that even though they'd lost all the elms years ago. It was endless, aimless talking, but he listened to it each morning anyway.

Dominic's days were like that until that one hot, humid Sunday in August when it finally happened.

He was ushering the eleven o'clock Mass with his buddy Herman. Herman sometimes clipped his fingernails during the service, the *click* echoing off the high polished marble walls, but Dominic figured he was a reliable usher and you could forgive him that. After seating the congregation, Dominic sat in the row reserved for ushers, the one in front marked off with a gold braided rope. It was a hot, humid, sweat-under-your-armpits kind of morning, and the church was packed. When Dominic decided to limp up the aisle and prop open the big wooden doors at the back of the church, he noticed the storm clouds forming to the west. He loved those oak doors, eight feet high and so thick they could stop a bullet. During idle moments of ushering, he used to stare at the intricate carvings on each panel: John the Baptist lifting water from the stream; the angel Gabriel appearing to the shepherds; the Resurrection of the Lord, his body surrounded by spokes of light filled with smooth knots.

Father Francis was saying the service, and just before the offertory, when he faced the altar and raised his hands toward the tall gilded spires and plaster statues of the gothic altar, a lightning ball appeared at the back of the church. Dominic was the first to see it because he was looking back toward the collection baskets, which he'd soon take aisle by aisle to collect the donations. The ball was bright white and fiery-looking and about the size of a basketball, with thin gossamer strands peeling off it. It hovered a few inches off the black and white marble floor. Then to Dominic's amazement, it began to roll, slowly, right down the center aisle of the church and toward the altar. It was like the ghost of something, or like the spot on your eye after you've looked into a flashbulb. Dominic nudged Herman, who seemed to take a quick gulp, his eyes bulging from his rotund face as if he'd just had a swallow of cheap schnapps.

Dominic watched the reaction of the parishioners as it passed them: the sudden open-mouthed gasps as if they'd just seen a miracle or witnessed a bad accident. Men in dark-gray suits and ties, women in their pastel Sunday dresses, the elderly clutching crystal rosaries in their frail hands all seemed to turn in unison, and a kind of wave moved, row by row, through the congregation. Standing for the offertory, their spines went stiff, like someone just dropped ice cubes down the backs of their Sunday shirts or blouses. Maybe some of them feared the ball would suddenly veer sideways, pick their aisle at random and stab them with a lightning bolt. Dominic was sure, by their panicky expressions, that some thought of slipping into the side aisle before the ball got there and rushing out the back archway of the church, but they couldn't take that first step.

Dominic wondered what would happen if someone came in contact with the lightning ball as it passed, whether or not it would electrocute them right on the spot, sending a sudden jolt of electricity into their bodies as if they'd touched a downed power line. As it got close to him, he thought about jabbing it with his finger; but he just froze, afraid to reach out toward it, and a little afraid not to.

As it passed, he could feel the hairs on the back of his hand stand up, which, Herman told him later, is a sign that lightning is about to strike you.

Then it dawned on Dominic that the lightning ball was headed right toward the altar; it looked as though it might roll up to the communion rail and bounce right up to Father Francis, and for a moment he wondered if he should shout out "Father! Father, look out!" or if he should just chuckle at the lightning ball. After all, he *was* sitting in church, and it was probably as harmless as the static cling in your socks.

The lightning ball paused there, in front of the communion rail, as if deciding, or as if waiting for some confessions from the sinners attending Mass that morning. By then it was so quiet in the church that the only sound you could hear was the rustle of Father Francis's gold and silver vestments as he raised and lowered his arms. It almost hurt Dominic's eyes to look at that brightness, the pale threads spinning off it as though it were rotating in place, a bright white tire spinning on glare ice.

Then the strangest thing happened: as if it had made its point, it reversed direction and began rolling steadily back up the aisle. Everyone, still standing and rigid like they were carved from wood, watched it pass the rows one by one as it made its way toward the back of the church and out the door.

At that moment, Father Francis, who had his back to the pews as he recited the Latin prayers that nobody understood, turned to the congregation. A frown spread over Father's face as he saw that no

119

one was paying attention to the service, that people were looking toward the back of the church, gasping or muttering or shaking their heads. Dominic figured, by the way his face turned red, that he wanted to chide the congregation for their inattentive behavior, for the way they couldn't focus on his wonderful service. He must have thought, at that moment, that the whole congregation was fallen away.

And he'd find out later that no one had donated money that day, since everyone was petrified, and Dominic and Herman didn't dare take the collection with those baskets with the velvet lining that always silenced the coins.

* * *

There was talk in the town about the lightning ball incident, and the townspeople argued at the Rainbow Café and on WKOS. Some said it was a holy sign, since it did, after all, appear in the aisle of the house of God on a Sunday morning. Others said that since it was made of fire, it was obviously an evil sign, maybe of the Devil himself, and that people had better repent before something terrible happened. After listening for a couple hours, Dominic had the urge to call the radio station on Monday morning, just to clear his mind, but when he picked up the phone and put it toward his lips, he realized he couldn't really find the words he needed to say. What he felt was that this whole lightning ball thing showed how the town got religion, or lost it, or maybe something in between. But what good would saying that do, he reasoned, except confuse the issue even more? And how could one simple man like him put that into a few words for the whole world? How would that small alphabet—just twenty-six letters—serve him then?

* * *

He replayed the church scene in his head all that day; wondering what it meant, what he was supposed to do to change, or if he *should* change at all. Maybe it was just a lightning ball—nothing more, nothing less. Just some freak thing that happens when the atmosphere is right. Maybe it was just some static electricity that packed itself into a sphere and, for no reason in particular, decided to roll down the aisle of a church.

He pondered the lightning ball into the evening until near ten o'clock, when he realized it was time to go up to bed. Would he recite his Our Father again, he wondered, or would he say something else? He reached up and switched on his 60-watt bulb on the porch. There was always a good reason for turning the light on, he thought. Its soft glow lit the porch and part of the yard each night, pushing the darkness back a little bit, in case there was trouble, or maybe someone in need.

BUD

The Things You Lose—
An Elusive Kind of Light

When you're an older ballplayer, like he is, what you lose is not your old glove, that glove you used each season from little league to high school until its leather fused with your flesh. Even though it was left in a sagging box in the attic, or maybe forgotten on a dust-blown field somewhere, the glove is not what you lose.

What you lose is not that faded Honus Wagner baseball card, passed down from someone's dad, then traded from kid to kid on playgrounds. What you lose is not that old card, kept in a shirt pocket until your mother washed it, and the card disappeared, shred by fibrous shred, into the soapy water swirling down the drain.

What you lose is not that fat-barreled Babe Ruth model bat you stumbled on as you walked the weeds at the edge of your neighborhood field. After you cracked the bat on an inside pitch, you pounded a nail into the thin handle, then taped it with masking tape, bandaging it carefully, like a broken ankle bone. One day when you came back from tech school and opened the garage door, you noticed a new set of shelves in the corner where the bat always leaned. You think you've lost it, but what you lose is not that bat.

What you lose is not your high school *League Champs* T-shirt, a shirt that shrunk smaller and smaller each year, tightening its grip around your waist and shoulders, a T-shirt that sprung holes in front and back, holes that grew larger and larger as if the shirt were gradually eating itself alive.

What you lose is not that state championship game you replay in your mind for thirty years. It's not that pitch you keep seeing, the pitch you should have hit, the baseball's seams always pink as stitch marks from a scar that won't heal. It's not that looping fly ball that falls in front of you, sinking slowly, like a coin dropped just beyond your fingertips into a deep lake. It's not those moments, though sometimes they circle painfully in your brain, like limping, injured dogs.

When you're an old ballplayer, what you lose is not that vacant lot where you played, a small field with a wooden home plate with a bare oval of dirt worn around it. What you think you lose is that small wood-slat fence at the edge of the field, and the row of pine trees, and beyond it, a field of tall grass that, as you stood there staring, seemed to stretch across Minnesota and all the way across America.

What you think you lose is that field in the evening with the fireflies rising from the deep grass and into the air, their tiny yellow lights blinking at you as you tried in vain to catch one in your cupped hand. Every few seconds, they'd light up, but always somewhere else above the field. When you asked the man who walked by your side why fireflies glow when they're only insects, he said he didn't know, that it wasn't electricity, exactly, but a power we humans didn't understand, an elusive kind of light. As you walked home, he slid his arm around your shoulder and told you a story about how each tiny firefly is like the soul of a person.

123

The Things You Lose—An Elusive Kind of Light

That field is gone; an aluminum-sided rambler smothers home plate. You still have memories, but they aren't what eat away at you little by little, they aren't the real things you lose. There will always be gloves and cards and T-shirts and games and fields. The real thing you lose is more important than any of those.

What you really lose is the person who took you to that field each day, the person who always walked by your side. What you really lose is that act of lifting your baseball in the stillness of late afternoon and tossing it across the blue air between you and your father. What you really lose is that game of catch, that arcing connection between your hand and his hand. For hours, the ball wove back and forth, sewing your palm, from a distance, to his. You can replace all those other things, but what you really lose is that.

Decades later, something tells you to walk from your house at dusk to a field at the edge of town. You pause, seeing a few blinking lights above the grass. You believe your father could be there, in one of those faint, tiny lights—speaking to you in a flickering code you can't quite understand.

So you stroll toward the middle, surrounded by those tiny illuminations that glow yellow for an instant, then go dark, then glow yellow again, but always in a different place. And though you know how hard it would be to catch one, you still reach out with your cupped palm. You reach out, as if you believe, on this empty field, it would be that easy to grasp an elusive kind of light.

124

DUANE

The Car Circle

■ ■ Other people in town might be doing lawn work around their houses; other people might be pulling tiny green weeds from their flower beds or spraying dandelions with *WeedBeGone*— but not Duane Price. Other people, like his nearest neighbor, Virgil Swigert, who's retired from working at the grain elevator, might be standing there in white gardening gloves, staring at the slow growth of zucchini or bell peppers or the inflating red balloons of tomatoes; they might be imagining the dull skin of potatoes beneath the brown dirt. But Duane Price sits up late at night, thinking about the streamlined bodies of old Fords and Chevys in the broad field behind his salvage yard, thinking about the way they're planted, trunk down, or balanced just right. He's thinking he only needs two more cars to add to the circle before he's finished. Duane Price has a dream: to build a replica of the stone structures of Stonehenge in England, except Duane wants to build his monument with salvaged cars. *It can be done,* he often tells himself as he sits at a card table and ponders a black-and-white photo of Stonehenge. *Anything a human being sets their mind to can be done.*

*   *   *

Because Duane owns Rite Away Auto, the salvage yard at the edge of Cosmos, he has all the supplies he needs for this project he's been calling Car Circle. Out in back, he has rows and rows of cars just sitting there, waiting. Some evenings he walks up and down the aisles as a king walks among his minions, as a Druid high priest strolls past his assistants. The cars wind up in his salvage yard for a lot of reasons: some cars slid through intersections and slammed into other cars, some rolled over in the ditch off County 66, and other cars just plain died on the road one fine day, their owners sputtering and swearing and slamming the dash with their fists as they cranked and cranked the key in the silent ignition. That's the thing about cars, Duane knows—they don't last forever. Rust takes over, friction takes over, the gears wear down to stubs, the transmission goes, and they're dead, plain and simple. When Duane drags a '68 Fairlane from the row, sprays it with rustproofing, and then plants it trunk down in his car circle, the car is reborn and resurrected, its fenders rising proudly toward the sky, its cracked headlights pointing heavenward.

Tonight, Duane sits at his card table—which he uses as a desk, even though one leg is a little too short and the table wobbles—and reads books about Stonehenge while he sips a Grain Belt beer. Since he was a boy, he's admired the mysterious English site, those thirty-eight balanced stone monoliths—some weighing thirty to forty tons—rising seventeen feet into the air. He's read all the theories about the ancient Druids and their magic, about how they used the stone structure to calculate the passage of another year, how they performed ceremonies in it to assure a good growing season, how they used it to determine the solstice. He's been amazed by the fact that they had a sight-line through the stones so you could look to the midsummer sunrise. But the solstice isn't all that important in the little town of Cosmos, Minnesota in the year 2006. The solstice doesn't matter all that much, as it did to the ancients in England. It comes, it goes, and it's just another day in June; the townspeople eat their sandwiches in Courthouse Park by the beds of cosmos flowers, and travelers, on their way to somewhere else, just pull in to the Town's Edge Quick Mart in their BMWs or SUVs, buy a foamy cup of cappuccino and a bag of Cheetos, and then head back toward the interstate.

Duane leans back in his undershirt, which always sticks to the metal of the card table chair, gazes up at his very first drawing of Car Circle—a crudely sketched pencil drawing of cars tipped on end, which he's laminated and tacked to the wall. He started on it five years ago, the day after he cut back on his business and went into semi-retirement. When he began building the structure during his free time, Duane decided that the old Fords would be the best cars to use. He had plenty of junked Fords in his salvage lot, and those '50s and '60s–era models were solid—long and low and square at the front and the hood—perfect for balancing another car on the top. Duane knows that Henry Ford was a great inventor with his Model T and all, but, in his opinion, the whole concept didn't really reach its pinnacle until the 1969 Ford Galaxie. *Such a beautiful beast,* Duane thinks as he considers its streamlined fenders and its crisscrossed grille and its long chrome strips stretching from head-light to taillight. *It's a work of art,* he thinks, *Every bit as pretty as a Rembrandt or a Picasso. And so is Car Circle.*

"It's a dumb idea," his wife Betty says to him from the living room, where she's watching TV, which they just hooked up to a new satellite dish. "You could be spending your spare time on something worthwhile." Lately, Betty's been selling the used jewelry she bought at garage sales on EBay.

"Like what?" he asks, squinting one eye in his pudgy face. "Like what?"

"Like clearing out the shed," Betty says, pursing her lips, "Or teaching Sunday school or something."

Duane knows Betty's hitting him below the belt, because he hasn't been to St. Stanislaus Church lately. He used to attend the church all the time, and was even in Usher's Club, but he hasn't gone for the last five or six years. Sure, he'd go to church, and he'd say the prayers during Mass and listen to Father Francis's sermon, but church just didn't give him anything; he didn't seem to see the light like other folks did. His voice was always scratchy and off-key during the hymns. And when he'd walk through the heavy oak doors and into the bright early morning sunlight, he'd feel empty. The stone steps—which were supposed to be solid—felt hollow beneath his feet as he walked down them and back to his car, skipping the Knights of Columbus all-you-can-eat pancake and sausage breakfast in the church basement. He knew that even if he stuffed himself with stacks of those syrup-covered pancakes, he'd still feel sort of hollow. He didn't know what it was, but lately a lot of things made him feel that way.

What really filled up his life were thoughts of his sculpture project. Once he finishes it, Duane plans to advertise it, maybe print a small flier to hand out to the tourists at the Cosmos Chamber of Commerce, though he wouldn't charge any money to see it. *Car Circle: Most Unique Attraction in Cosmos, Minnesota.* Maybe he'll even string some lights across the field so the cars could be illuminated at night. Tourists can come and go as they please, viewing one of the most amazing sights in the Midwest, in North America even. Maybe Car Circle will fill the tourists with a feeling of wonder they haven't had for a while, and that would be enough for Duane.

128   *   *   *

"What about when them cars start to go?" Otto Grosshans asks Duane down at the Rainbow Café the next morning. Otto's the proprietor of the Rainbow, sometimes wears a red International Harvester cap to cover his bald head, and he's always the skeptic.

"What do you mean?" Duane asks. Duane knows there are lots of naysayers in town; he knows people are buzzing about his Car Circle. A few of them call it art, others call it whimsy, and a lot of others say it's just plain junk.

"Rust. That's what I'm talking about. What about when the damn cars rust out? The whole thing will topple down."

"It'll never happen," Duane says, defensively clacking his coffee cup onto the small china plate. "Not my cars. I've got them rust-proofed and wired solid. Some have steel support beams to boot."

"But eventually . . . ," Otto says. "I mean, after fifty or a hundred years, you won't even *be* here, and the rust. . . ."

"Aw, what the hell do you know?" Duane says abruptly, anger welling up inside and pushing the words out. He hates the word *rust.* Duane quickly slurps the last of his coffee, slides a quarter on the Formica countertop for the waitress, does a half-spin on his vinyl stool, and saunters out of the café.

Agitated by Otto's comments, he hurries home and makes a bee-line toward the salvage yard, past Swigert's garden, where he can see old man Swigert bent over a sprouting plant. Every day, Duane sees Virgil working on his garden; some days he stays out there on his hands and knees until dusk, sweating and pulling weeds. It's like he's tied to a stake in that garden. "Gonna be a real good crop this year," tall, gaunt Swigert bragged to Duane earlier that spring. "Biggest red peppers in the county. You wait and see." Dirt smudges decorated his faded tan safari-style shirt.

Duane crosses the field toward his cars, and just being near Car Circle calms him down. It's his Garden of Eden. The big long cars leap up from the soft sandy soil like kids jumping up from the lake water after they've been holding their breaths for a long time. He knows when he'll add those two cars to finish the circle: June twenty-first will be the day—the solstice, the first day of summer. The twenty-first falls on a Sunday this year. That's the moment—at dawn—when Duane plans to complete Car Circle.

Then, first thing Monday morning, he'll call the local media and chamber of commerce and maybe even Channel 5 over in Minneapolis so everybody knows. He's not calling them for the publicity or the fame. He's just calling them because it's there, it's finished, it's done. It's Car Circle.

After dinner, Duane sits at the card table and gazes at one of his drawings.

"Come watch TV with me, will you, Duane?" Betty says from the living room couch, the one they got at the new Furniture Barn. "*In Search of . . .* is on."

"Not right now," he replies. "I was just going out back to check my cars."

"They're not going any place," Betty says. "Your cars can wait, can't they?"

129

"No they can't." Duane grabs the drawing and walks to the hall closet to get his jacket.

After a long pause, Betty purses her lips, then says, "Duane, I'm beginning to get scared."

Duane stops in his tracks on the green shag carpet of their small rambler. "Of what?"

"I mean, this Car Circle thing is going too far."

"Too far? I'm not even *finished* with it yet."

Betty gathers herself with a deep breath. "What I mean is that you're *thinking* about it too much. I'm afraid you're going crazy. You know, you're sixty-six years old. It could be Alzheimer's setting in or something."

Duane looks down at the pencil drawing in his hand, like a Leonardo Da Vinci sketch with lines and vectors, only cruder, with less symmetry. "Who's *not* going crazy?" he finally replies. "Show me one man my age in Cosmos who's not crazy in one way or another."

Betty strolls over to Duane, slides her pudgy arms around his shoulders. "Come on, Duane. Just watch the show with me, just this once. Your project can wait."

"It's June nineteenth already."

"So?"

"So, I only have a couple of days to get it done."

Betty looks into his eyes, pouting for a few seconds.

"Okay, okay," he finally says with a half-smile, "I'll watch."

"Just like we used to." She sits on the sofa, holds out a dish of Chex Mix for him to snack on.

"Yeah, like we used to," he agrees, sitting down, tossing a handful of tiny pretzels into his mouth.

They watch the rerun of *In Search of . . .* that features a segment on the lost tombs of Egypt and the mysteries of the great pyramids. "The pyramids were built because human beings longed to be closer to the sky," Leonard Nimoy says. "They believed the steps of the pyramids brought them closer to the gods." As they watch, Duane slides his arm around Betty and pulls her close to him. He knows Betty's right—the cars can wait. Still, that comment Otto made about the rust bothers him, and he keeps hearing it in the back of his mind all through the TV show.

*　　*　　*

Hours later, long after Betty is asleep, Duane slips from bed, pulls on his undershirt and overalls, and quietly descends the stairway.

Outside, he follows the trail in the tall grass that leads past old man Swigert's garden. Duane walks near those even rows of dirt with the plants growing from them; he can see, in the moonlight, the tiny green zucchini, the small bubbles of red peppers sprouting.

Duane looks across the field to the circle of cars, their curving lines. He's made the structure to replicate the exact size and shape of the seventeen-foot monolithic stones in England. *What did they mean?* He wonders. *Who built them out there in the open field in 4000 B.C.? How did they haul those thirty-ton pieces of sandstone to the Salisbury Plain, dragging them across marshes and moors and up hillsides?* He read in one article that the survivors of the Druids still practice their religious magic; on certain days, they hold ceremonies at the historic Stonehenge site.

Before he crosses the field, Duane strolls the aisles among the junked cars, lined in rows behind his salvage shop, sees the crumpled hoods, the crack-filled windshields. Sees the smashed side doors from some T-bone crash at the county intersection. Then he sees the Galaxie. It's Robin's-egg blue, with long, chrome strips; the car's body is in good shape, since the pistons just locked up and quit one day. As he stares at it, it seems like the headlights flare a little at him. Or, he wonders, is that just a reflection from a car passing on the county road?

The next thing he knows, he's sitting inside the car. The car transforms into every car Duane's ever owned. He smells the scent of new vinyl, the clean cloth upholstery, the air freshener shaped like a pine tree dangling from the visor. He checks his rearview mirror, sees his hair, thicker, bushier, not balding. Or is that just a shadow? No matter—he floors the accelerator, and the landscape blurs past him like it did when he was sixteen and just got his license. Like it did that first night when he wanted to see how it felt to go a hundred miles an hour. Like it did when he was young and free and not tied to this salvage business. The work's okay, but the part about it he hates is when the police call him to the site of an accident. There, his tow truck pulls the hissing, steaming wrecks off the highway, and sometimes he gets a glimpse of fresh bloodstains on the cloth seats. Right

131

now he feels like he did fifty years ago, when a five-dollar bill in his pocket was enough—he wasn't chained to a lease on this land, scrimping just to make the payments.

"Duane," a voice calls. It's a faraway voice from a teenaged girl, a girl he met in high school decades ago, a girl named Betty who always spoke his name as if she were singing it. "Duane," the voice says again, louder, pulling him from his trance. It *is* Betty, who's standing by the side of the Galaxie in her pink bathrobe.

Duane stares at her in surprise.

"You woke me when you got out of bed," she says. "Why are you out here?"

Duane opens the driver's side door and slips out. Without a word, moving as though he's in a dream, he opens the creaking back door of the Galaxie, grabs her hand and pulls her in. Betty gasps. He slides the bathrobe off her shoulders, exposing her pale blue nightgown, then peels that layer back, exposing the soft creamy skin of her shoulder. Betty lets out a girlish giggle, enjoying his attention.

Duane lowers his lips to kiss the nape of her neck. Her neck is warm and moist, and it tastes like lavender and Turtle Wax. For half an hour, in the soft illuminated glow of the moonlight, they make love on the velour seat of the Galaxie. Later, Duane lies on his back, Betty's head resting on his chest, the roof of the Galaxie above them like a soft cloth sky. "Love," he sighs, finally answering her question.

"What?" she whispers, her eyelids half closed.

"Love. That's why I'm out here in this car. For love."

* * *

On June twenty-first, in the moonlit field at 3 a.m., Duane is ready for the final piece of his puzzle. A flashlight clenched in his leather work glove, he checks the angle of the cars one more time, studies his drawings and notes. The night is perfect—silent, no breeze, stars like a million points of iron filings piercing the black sky. In the west, a yellow moon paints a glow over the rounded fenders of Car Circle. Their chrome grins faintly. Duane gazes at the sculpture. *Old Otto is full of bull,* he thinks as he recalls their conversation in the café. *This thing will last a thousand years, at least. Ten thousand maybe. A million.* Then he glances over at Virgil Swigert's garden, sees his steady, boring rows, pictures small tomatoes balancing on the vines. He shakes his head, thinking that, in a few hours, Virgil will be out there with his white gardening gloves, pulling weeds one by one by one.

Duane hops into the small pay-loader, starts it, and drives over to the '69 Galaxie, the last link in his Car Circle. He knows exactly where it must go—on top of those two level Fords on the east side of the circle. He tenderly connects the chains to the Galaxie's bumper and chassis, making sure they won't pull loose, then drags it slowly across the field toward the circle. In the cab of the crane, Duane fires up the engine, the puff of black smoke rising from the exhaust pipe. He moves the crane's control levers, lifting the Galaxie steadily, without wavering, then gently, gently lowers it. He thinks for a moment about the ancients in England, somehow placing the huge, multi-ton rocks on top of the Stonehenge circle. *How did they do it?* he wonders for a second. *Was it sheer will? Was it love? Or was it magic, pure and simple?*

As the Galaxie comes to rest on the other cars, its chassis creaks a little, and Duane can see the cars sway slightly beneath its fifteen hundred–pound weight. Climbing out of the crane, he figures he'll wire the Galaxie onto the other cars later; for right now, he'll sit down on the grass, admire his work, and wait for the sunrise, which will happen in about an hour. He'll watch it rise at the perfect angle, in the narrow space between two cars, just like the ancients did with their monoliths at Stonehenge. *Were they crazy, just like me?* he wonders. *Or did they just have faith? Did they know there are things that are much more important than our petty little lives?* He looks across the field at the back window of his house, thinks he sees an oval shape, a face rising in that window. Is it Betty, watching him? Is it the glow of her loving face? After all these years, though she sometimes doubted him, she let him go ahead with his dream. She let him take thousands of pounds of scrap metal and turn it into something beautiful. He plans to bring her out here after dawn to see his masterpiece, finally finished.

Anticipating the horizon brightening with that dark red color, Duane feels excitement filling him from the inside. Though he's only wearing overalls and a tattered undershirt, he could be dressed in

133

dark Druid's robes, he could be a high priest standing at an altar, waiting for a message from the stars and planets, waiting to pass that message to the people of the village. *The message is*, thinks Duane, *one man can accomplish whatever he wants, one man can chase a goal, and eventually he'll catch up to it.* Suddenly he feels like a person who's been blind all his life, and now, in the first light of the solstice, is finally going to see.

All the thoughts in Duane's head make it feel suddenly heavy, so he closes his eyes a few seconds, tips his head back in the grass. The next thing he knows, a form floats across the lawn near the house. It appears to be a pale blue nightgown, hovering a few inches off the dark lawn, and it's moving gracefully toward him.

At that moment something begins on the far side of the field, near the silhouettes of the tall trees. Duane can hear it, like a hissing sound, coming from somewhere near old man Swigert's garden. The sound approaches, wave-like, ruffling the field. The sound rises in pitch as it rushes through the long swaying grass, and Duane realizes that it's the first wind of the morning, raising its head. It's the first gust of wind before dawn, moving toward him as a layer of warm air meets a layer of cold. When the wind reaches him, it swirls around him, buffing his face, fluttering his overalls. For an instant Duane thinks he hears a distant cry—a voice, a creaking sound, calling his name, and he looks up to see the Galaxie above him, rocking ever so slightly in the wind, as if it's thinking about losing its balance. Beyond it, the whole sky glows rust-red and beautiful. Then he recognizes the voice of the woman in the nightgown as she gets closer, a voice calling and calling him urgently, the way you call a person in the morning who overslept, trying to wake them from a deep dream.

134

ELMO

The Groundskeeper

So much depends on his small baseball field, set between the green rows of the cornfield and the pale stones of the cemetery. So much depends on the way he tends the grass, watering it and watering it on the last days of summer, so it burns green as long as it possibly can. He waters it until, as he walks across them, the grass blades reach up with thin fingers to touch the leather soles of his work boots. No matter if the people in town call him just an old weirdo, he knows a lot depends on the way he lays that white chalk line along the third and first baselines; he knows if he wavers the slightest bit, fair becomes foul, foul fair.

The little leaguers from town can run onto the field at any time and it'll be ready, waiting for them. There are no bad hops on his field—it's hard enough to catch a whirring grounder without it hitting a rut, taking a vicious hop toward the face. It's hard enough to run back to the wall for a long drive without a hollow spot pulling the earth out from under you, throwing you off. Balance: that's Elmo's credo. Balance and leveling and balance.

The townspeople say he's obsessed with this field. He could brag about the place, but he doesn't. He could say Cosmos Memorial Field is the best-kept field in the Midwest, but he doesn't—he just tends the field alone, with no one watching. He pounds nails into the warped boards of the outfield fence, straightening them, then covers them with a coat of whitewash. He rakes the soil around the batter's box until it's smooth as the stretched blue sky above it. He knows, as he grooms it, that he's only touching the surface, the skin of the soil. He knows the soil he touches goes deep into the earth where no mere man could ever reach: it goes all the way to the soul of this planet. At least that's what his father told him once as they sat in the grandstand. His father learned it from his father. Elmo's father and grandfather were groundskeepers too, tending the same grass on this field in the town where all three of them grew up.

Once in a while, at dusk, after he finishes his jobs, he gets the impulse to run the bases, imagine the cheering in his ears as if he's just hit a home run that wins the World Series. But, at sixty-eight, he's too old to run like that. Instead, he sometimes drops to his knees in the middle of the diamond and gives thanks for the millions of grass blades, for the chance to water them, keep them green this long into the drought.

He knows some of the townspeople make fun of him, especially Eddie Comstock and his two buddies. They say he takes his job too seriously for what it's worth. But exactly what *is* it worth? He'll tell you what: inside those rickety wooden fences, rounded to 400 feet at their furthest point, 330 feet down the lines, is grass so green you'd swear it would live forever. Inside those fences is a diamond that, if you looked down and spotted it from one of those jetliners heading to Minneapolis, you'd say is just right in its symmetry.

On the north side of the ball field, next to St. Stanislaus Church, sits the town cemetery, and he tends that, too. He pushes a mower between the gravestones carefully, so as not to disturb the dead, so the place stays neat in case the living want to come to visit. Sometimes he pauses and stands in front of his father's headstone, which has been there for ten years. Next to it is his grandfather's. If he pauses too long there, feeling the vibrations in the hollow handle of the mower, the exhaust starts to burn his eyes and make them water, so he just has to move on.

"You know you don't have to mow the cemetery," Father Francis often tells him. "You don't have to tend the graves. We could hire someone."

"I mow it because I want to, that's all," he answers. He figures you have to find the things you like to do, small as they might be, and then just go ahead and do them.

He loves to begin mowing at the outside edge of the pitcher's mound, and mow around and around, the way his father taught him. Each circle surrounds the one he's just mowed. Sometimes when he's finished, he climbs to the top row of the bleachers and gazes out at the nap of the grass, carved in a spiral. And he thinks *Yep, that's it, all right.* He thinks about how you start with one small circle, then make a second one, a little larger than the one before. He thinks about how, eventually, you could mow around the whole earth that way, circles around circles. All the while, almost without your knowing, the sun circles across the sky and the earth circles around the sun. It's then that he realizes how tiny he is, how humble we all should be, and how he's not much different than a single blade of grass circled by billions.

*   *   *

But not everyone is humble. Some people think the world is so small they could smash it in their hands like a piece of clay. Some nights at the Wander Back Tavern, guys like Eddie Comstock remind Elmo of that. Eddie sneers up at him from under the shadow of his greasy ball cap, then stares back at his hand of cards, always a little bent at the corners. After a few beers, Eddie starts in on him, saying "Hey Elmo, why aren't you out there cutting the grass with a fingernail clipper?" He lets out a laugh, which, after smoking half a pack of Marlboros, scrapes from his throat. "Yeah," his friends chime in, "Hey old school, why aren't you out there praying for the grass?"

These guys are a few years out of high school, and they work at the Rainbow Quarry, shoveling and loading gravel. They never fail to talk about how their work is a pain in the ass. Friday and Saturday nights, with nowhere to go, they hang out at the Wander Back, playing Sheepshead and shaking dice and flexing their muscles as they lift pitchers of beer. Sometimes, for no particular reason, they start fights in the bar, especially with the Mexicans who work as crop pickers.

As usual, Elmo ignores their comments and orders a Grain Belt, which he gets, along with a sympathetic nod from Duane, the rotund bartender who's an older man, too. Elmo realizes these young guys just don't understand the life of a groundskeeper. They don't know he's seen a lot of dry years when the sky held back on the rain for weeks, and he had to be out there morning and night with his sprinklers. They couldn't imagine the parched dry taste in his throat those summers. They haven't been through the wet years, when the water pools around home plate and third base, and he had to cart in wheelbarrows full of dry sand just to make the infield playable for Bud Walden's Cosmos Comets squad. They don't remember those years or carry them around deep inside the way Elmo does.

"Hey Elmo, how come you don't answer?" goads Eddie. "Why aren't you out there saying your prayers?"

He starts to burn as they keep it up, and he wants to burst out with "Maybe you boys should be doing something worthwhile;" but instead he says his usual, which is nothing. He just takes a slow sip of beer and gazes behind the bar at the photos of the town's championship amateur teams, the trophies glimmering next to them. He knows Eddie and his pals were never worth a damn as ball players; they never played on the team, like some of the local boys.

* * *

Later, as he leaves the tavern and walks back past the darkened field, he hears it: the growl of an engine in the parking lot behind the grandstands, voices cackling, a sound like tin cans clanking. Then he sees the headlights flare near the far side of the field as someone dashes over and yanks the gate open. He hustles though the gate by the dugout and freezes there, eyes fixed on the car that pulls onto the grass near the right-field line, engine revving. *Jesus,* he thinks he says with a gasp, though he doesn't hear the word come out. *Jesus!* It stings his eyes to see the car spin a circle in his grass, carving grooves with its rear tires. The headlights circle themselves as the car roars, its back end rotating. He flinches, feeling each gouge in the sod as surely as someone is scraping his skin with a dull knife.

Breaking from his trance, he unlocks the storage shed, pulls out an old Louisville Slugger, and hurries onto the field. The car idles a few seconds, its exhaust rising into the red glow of its taillights.

The engine snarls and the car accelerates right at him, faster and faster. He supposes they figure he's going to turn and run, and for an instant, he thinks he is, too. But he just holds his ground. His wiry body gathers all the strength from those years of hefting wheelbarrows and bags of chalk lime and mountains of dirt, and he just holds his ground. The car speeds toward him, its lights steady, not jostling at all on the surface of the grass he's taught to be so smooth. Just a few yards from him, the car brakes and swerves, the fender sliding closer and closer to him. He wavers a little as the car finally comes to a stop just a few feet from him, and the engine kills.

Fists clenched on that Louisville Slugger, he squints at the grinning faces in the darkened car, illuminated by the amber light of the dash. It's no secret who's inside that low-riding, dented red Pontiac. Their rapid-fire laughter echoes off the fences.

Elmo is a peaceful man, and he always has been; he's always kept to himself. But when he thinks of the burning scars the tires have cut on the beautiful green of center field, it finally gets to him. He can almost hear that field, that innocent field, crying out to him in pain. It's then that maybe he does go a little crazy, like they've been saying.

Standing in front of the car, he rears back with his skinny arms and, like a ball player stepping into a fast ball right down the heart of the plate, he takes a quick, hard swing with the bat. The left headlight bursts with a hollow pop. The laughter inside the car stops. "Hey, damn it!" Eddie's voice calls, "The hell you doing?" *I'm doing what I need to,* he thinks as he moves to the other side of the car, swings the bat and the other headlight explodes. Inside, Eddie, looking stunned, curses Elmo as he grinds the ignition and the car turns over a few times with a gravelly sound until the engine finally

139

catches. Elmo glares at the blind eye sockets of the headlights as the car backs away.

*   *   *

After they've gone he looks out in disbelief at the circular ruts, and he can't stop his whole body from shaking, can't stop his heart from squeezing and squeezing its fist inside his chest. He stands there for a long time, gazing at his ruined field, afraid to walk out to access all the damage. One thing he knows for sure—he'll carry these scars around with him for a long time.

He thinks for a moment about those boys, pities them for their cruelty, for whatever anger coiled inside them so long that they had to do this. And then another thought seeps in; he's upset by the boys and their car, and by something else, too. He's always believed that so much depends on this field, but right now he realizes that, no matter how much he tends it, the field won't last forever; it's not perfect and he can't keep it that way. It's just grass. Just fragile blades of grass.

He tilts his head toward the clouded sky, and the first drops of rain touch his face, gently at first. Then it begins to rain harder, soaking his tan shirt and pants, soaking the field and the ugly gouges left by the thick treads of the tires. Wisps of steam rise from the raw, dark earth as the cool water lands on it.

It's then that he falls to his knees. He reaches down and presses his palm into one of the ruts. Along its edge, he sees the tiny, exposed roots. He caresses them with his fingertips, and as he does he can almost feel them, already beginning to grow.

140

CHANCE

The Crop Duster

What I like most about this job is flying just under the telephone wire, that false horizon that divides the swaying green crops from the endless blue. I maneuver the plane just right, wings steady so they cut the space between the black wire and the damp ground. Then I'm up again, the sky licking me with its broad blue tongue. With each swoop I deliver a cloud of pesticide that broadens and settles over the crops so shoppers can lift their perfect, unmarred tomatoes or bell peppers from the grocery shelves of the Cosmos Market.

But that's not the real reason I do this: I fly because most men my age lie on a couch and stare at reruns on ESPN. I fly because most men my age can't do a three-sixty in the sky. No one can do that as gracefully as I can, banking above the acres with a slow roll of my double wings, turning earth on its back and sky on its nose.

When you fly, your leaden, five hundred pound machine rises impossibly high off the ground, and you stay there as long as you can, your propeller surprising the air. After years of being a crop duster, you learn just how to adjust the wings so you pass untouched, halfway between the sizzling wires and the dull, waiting earth. You pass through that middle and toward the other side of the field, where you barrel-roll with delight, and in that reverie maybe it doesn't matter if you don't know up from down for a few seconds, earth from sky: maybe the two of them just merge into one, and that's okay.

"It's just a daydream," she says to me, "isn't it?"

I don't really know how to answer her, how to explain this feeling I get when I pull the throttle back and watch the tiny black needles in those gauges jump from their slumber. I don't really know how to tell her that I love it up there so much I never want to come down, even at dusk, when any sane-minded crop duster would be grounded and sitting inside a sheet-metal hanger with his goggles around his neck and a 16-ounce bottle of Sprite in his hand. It's hard to resist the roar of the propeller, the close calls of the wings as they narrowly miss the trees and the splintered sides of paint-chipped barns. Each day I dodge the obstacles, outrun the danger. I surprise the sunset with my wings, I startle the horizon with my quick banking turns. I startle gravity with my lift.

142

"You don't have wings, really," she tells me.

I just stare at her a long time when she says that, a little surprised by the sharpness of her honesty.

"You try to be so different than anyone else. But deep down, you're not. You just work in the produce department of a grocery. You know you don't have wings."

And I sit my silence, my loud, loud silence, and lower the puffy lids of my eyes as if I were a man falling asleep.

"And you don't either," I finally say back to her.

"I never claimed to," she replies, her half-smile reminding me of the curve of a wing that gives it lift.

*   *   *

I know the power lines could do me in, and I know I really don't have to fly beneath them, but I do anyway. If I did hit a wire, the electricity would leap through the metal steering wheel, and I imagine I'd feel a sudden waking jolt as surely as if I was a man sleepwalking in an open field in the middle of a thunderstorm. For now, I love the steady balance of wings, the wire slicing above me like the blade of a cheese cutter, the quick blur of the gray telephone poles in the periphery of each eye. Precision, that's what I'm about. To my way of thinking, it's a test of skill, just as the pro quarterback or the gymnast or the slalom skier's skills are tested, just as the surgeon's scalpel, as it slices carefully along the cauliflower-shaped lobes of the brain, is tested each day.

* * *

Reclining in the front seat of the car, we watch the drive-in movie where the couples—Gary Cooper and Vivian Leigh or maybe Clark Gable and Marilyn Monroe—are always about to kiss. They're still alive on that black-and-white screen, no matter how long they've been gone. They're young, and their age never catches up with them, and that's what's magical—and maybe a little scary—about watching a classic film. I reach toward her and our hands squeeze tightly together. We could be squeezing the whole world between them. "You give me wings," I say. It's every bit as romantic as what's happening on the 40-foot screen, every bit as real as that thunderstorm, boiling up on the flat horizon.

* * *

On the way home from the movie, I say, "Did I ever tell you my father was a crop duster? And his father before him?"

"So your dad wasn't really a traveling salesperson?"

"No, well . . . ," I reply. "He was one of those test pilots. He took an F-15 straight up into the stratosphere, just to see what would happen when it broke the sound barrier." I say this, though we both know my father sold kitchen gadgets for years, and that my grandfather plied leather in a shoe factory in southern Wisconsin.

She smiles a smile that says *I know you're a crazy dreamer, and it's all right.*

The Crop Duster

And I love her for letting me glide steadily through the air, then banking up, up, up where I don't feel the pull of the earth.

I love her for letting me walk out into this open field at night, the clouds tumbling forward from the horizon, the heat lightning illuminating their insides. There's never any thunder from heat lightning—it just flashes and flashes in the belly of a cloud, making it translucent for a split second. It's just an illusion of storm, and in that instant you think you see the very center of the cloud, its heart. Our lives are like that, I've come to believe: some quick flashes, and maybe you see the inside of it all, or maybe not.

*　　*　　*

I love it that she's next to me in this field, strolling like a sleepwalker as we amble through the grass that rises and falls around our ankles. When we reach the middle, I lean toward her for a kiss, and just before we touch I feel a tick of static electricity between our lips. She pulls back with a quick laugh that breaks the sound barrier. When she leans to kiss me again, her lips taste like a garden of fresh strawberries, fresh strawberries, fresh strawberries. It's then that we hear the steady hum of a small plane in the distance. We don't know where it's coming from or where it's headed, we just gaze at the way it defies gravity, the faint blinking jewels of its lights like some undiscovered constellation.

144

PART THREE

A ROAD SO CLOSE TO HOME

SKIP REMEMBERS

A Road So Smooth, and So Close to Home

"C'mon," my father said to me one warm spring evening after dinner, when I was fourteen. He led me out to the dirt-floored garage near the alley, and we climbed into the green Plymouth. The car's whole interior was covered with soft beige cloth— the dashboard, the sides of the doors, even the roof above our heads. When I was younger and riding with my father, I had always believed that if there was an accident, all that cloth padding would be enough to protect us from ever getting hurt. Dad had used the old Plymouth on his sales trips, which sometimes lasted three or four days, and I wondered why he wanted me to go out for a drive that night.

He only drove us a few blocks, then pulled into the parking lot of my old grade school. With the car idling in neutral, he hopped out of the driver's side, circled the car, and opened my door.

"What are you waiting for?" he said. "Slide behind the wheel." I hesitated, my fingertips burrowing into the upholstery. "You said you wanted to learn to drive sometime, didn't you?"

I grinned nervously and slid over. I knew nothing about driving, and the wheel of the Plymouth, encased in a green cloth wheel-cover, felt too wide in my hands. For a moment I just stared through the windshield at the corn stalks that silhouetted the parking lot.

Without giving me any instructions, Dad reached over with one foot, pushed in the clutch, and put the stick shift in first gear.

The car rocked forward.

I remember the panic of not knowing how to shift or what to do next. I drove small, rapid circles on the buckled asphalt.

I glanced at him helplessly.

"What now?" I pleaded.

"Just drive," he said.

"What?"

"That's the way I learned," he said. "Just drive."

*   *   *

During his traveling salesman days, my father got to know every type of road in south central Minnesota. He spent most of his time on the county roads with their cracked, cement surfaces. The worst, he told me, were the gravel roads. Gravel flew up and hit the underside of the car, making sounds like distant gunshots, and the car always arrived at the next town caked with dust.

He told me what he loved most about his job were those new county roads that were just resurfaced with asphalt. The faster he accelerated, the smoother the ride seemed to become. He loved the way the tires seemed to turn to pure air, and the car would glide without bumps or shivers, the pens he always kept on the dashboard no longer clinking together.

One evening, when I was four or five years old, he drove us outside town to a county road that was lined with cornfields. Dad sold feed for Nutrena in southern Minnesota and Iowa during those years, so he knew corn well. As far as I could see, the whole world was corn, endless fields of corn. "Let me show you something," he had said as we pulled up to a crossroads, and he stopped the car.

Then he pressed hard on the accelerator. He glanced anxiously at the dashboard, and his face tightened as if, inside his skin, someone was turning a steering wheel as far it would go. His back straightened and his body seemed to become sleeker as we sped faster and faster, until I thought the Plymouth was going to lift off the ground and fly. His eyes narrowed, his pupils black as the asphalt he stared at.

Finally he spoke, raising his voice over the whine of tires and the rushing air.

"Do you remember that nature show we watched on TV last week?"

"Yeah," I said, remembering the smooth black cheetah, world's fastest animal.

"Well I've been thinking about that," he said. "See this speedometer? We're going one hundred." He was almost shouting at me. "We're going as fast as that cheetah can run," he said.

* * *

I must have driven a dozen circles on the school parking lot. I waited for another direction from Dad. "Go ahead and shift," he said.

I pounded the clutch in, tried to find second. The gears gnawed at each other. "Up and forward," he instructed. "Up and forward."

I finally found the notch for the gear, and when I let out the clutch, the car lurched faster, then began jerking and shivering. "Give it more gas," Dad ordered.

I pushed the gas pedal half-way down and the next thing I knew, the car plowed into a stack of crates piled next to the school. We would have hit the building behind the boxes, but the car stopped with a thump just inches from the brick wall.

I looked down and saw my Dad's big foot on the brake.

With the sudden stop, I had lunged forward and hit my lip on the steering wheel. I touched my lip, and saw a red circle of blood on my fingertip.

"You all right?" Dad asked.

I didn't answer, just tipped my head back toward the cloth sky and thought *I'll never learn to drive a car like Dad, not ever.* That piece of machinery just seemed too huge and clumsy and complicated.

"You're not very good at this," he said. "But you'll learn."

We sat for a moment in the silence of the killed engine.

"You know," he said, his voice turning almost wistful, "I always thought you'd make a good salesman."

I looked at him incredulously. "Salesman?" I asked. I had never even considered it.

He looked through the windshield at the red bricks glowing in the low sun. "You have all the chances. Not like me when I started out. I was scrounging and struggling and sleeping in the car." I tasted the metallic taste of blood on my lip, touched it again with my finger.

"Here," he said. He leaned over and, with the sleeve of his white shirt, he dabbed my lip. "You okay?"

I nodded.

He leaned back. "Now let's start this thing. Find reverse and back it out of here," he said. "You'll learn to be a good driver. I know you will."

I stared at him for a moment and thought about the transformation he had made that time years earlier when he drove us as fast as a cheetah on the new asphalt road. "Think of it," he had said afterwards as we headed back to town. "A road so smooth. And so close to home." He glanced down at the speedometer needle, falling back to the speed limit. "If every road in the state was like that one," he sighed, "I could drive forever. You know what I mean?"

"Yeah," I said, though I wasn't quite sure what he meant.

I just knew that when we pulled up to the town's only stoplight, he gradually became my father again: paunchy in his white shirt, slightly balding, his feet too big for the pedals. He became the man who did not need to drive a hundred miles an hour, the man who did not need to accelerate forever in this car.

He was the man who would steer us onto our concrete driveway with the grass sprouting between the cracks. The man who, for years as he returned from his sales trips, would stop the car close to

150

the house, leave the keys jingling in the ignition, and lift me out with his large hands.

* * *

It took me a few tries after I started the car, but I found reverse and backed the car away from the wall and the wreckage of crates and boxes.

We drove around and around that parking lot until dusk, until I learned to shift and clutch and steer better than I ever thought I could, until the thin corn leaves darkened to asphalt black, like the lines branching across a county highway map.

Dad coached me that last half hour, his body poised slightly forward the whole time, one hand lightly clenched on the padded dash.

Whenever I glanced nervously toward him, all I kept seeing was the shirt sleeve on his left arm, the red circles of blood I knew would not wash out.

SKIP REMEMBERS

The Rescue

1

I know what it's like to have a son who follows rivers.

Last summer, as we walked along the river near our newly purchased house in Cosmos, my four-year-old son asked why the sunfish, lying on the bank, looked so still. I couldn't answer him, just stared at the bright yellow and blue markings, the translucent, motionless tail.

"Is it asleep?" he asked.

"Yes," I answered. "Maybe it is."

He nudged at it with the toe of his tennis shoe. "It can't be sleeping. Its eye is still open."

* * *

Now, in early winter, sometimes I put my face near the frosted upstairs window and stare for a long time across the Cosmos River, which, downstream, feeds into the Minnesota River and then into the Mississippi.

"Why are you always looking out at the river?" my son asks.

"Just thinking, I guess," I reply, knowing I haven't really answered his question. Deep down, I *do* know why I'm always staring out at the river. I'm worried about the ice, and small boys walking on it. Later, I tell my son about the newspaper article I read yesterday—about a boy who wandered onto the ice of the river. "He was four—the same age as you," I tell him. Then I explain how the boy fell through a hole in the ice and the strong current pulled him under.

A crew of divers looked for him for hours, but they never found the body. I imagined his parents, standing on the shore, their arms frozen around each other.

2

"What's it like to walk on the river in winter?" my son asks.

His question comes out of nowhere, while we're driving in the car.

I want to say it's strangely silent out there, though sometimes you think each footstep makes a loud noise. I want to tell him about the time my father and I went ice fishing on Lake Cosmos, how nervous I felt the first time we drove across the ice in the old Rambler. I was certain the car would fall through. When we parked in the middle of the lake, I touched my toe gently onto the ice, then hesitated, as though I were about to step on brittle window glass, as though the world would give way.

153

Instead, I just mutter "Don't ever try it," and I turn the steering wheel and ease us around the corner.

3

One day in February when the weather warms, my wife and I take our son on a walk near the river. The river's still coated with a white highway of ice, and its skin is healed over in the place where the boy fell through. We walk closer to feed the ducks that swim in the water where a narrow channel of the ice has melted. The ducks are ecstatic to be circling in this cold, murky water, and their green iridescent heads bob for bits of bread tossed to them by our son. "Not so near the river," we warn our son, and we try to grab his hand. But he won't hold our hands for long when we're close to the river. He's too excited by the first glimpse of water, the flurry of ducks all around him. When we're not paying attention, he takes a quick step onto a shelf of overhanging ice, and I rush to pull him back. As we walk back to the house, my wife and I scold him until he cries. Angry, we march him up the muddy hillside to the house and make him stay inside for the afternoon. He doesn't understand; for him, water is water, and ice is ice, and there's no world between the two.

4

We have a son who dreams of walking along rivers. A son who dreams of sliding down a white snow bank and into the river. He squeals with joy as the splash rises around him in a white crown. "I'm not cold," he says. He sees us, his mother and father, standing on the shore as he floats on a large cake of ice in the middle. "I'm not cold," he says, and waves to us as he floats downstream.

5

"They should find that little boy who drowned," he tells me before he goes to sleep one night. "They should find him and let his mommy and daddy bury him."

"They're still looking for him," I reply, imagining the boy, far downstream, still staring with wide, surprised eyes at the thin layer of December ice. Sometimes I wonder how close we all are to that kind of ice, the kind that gives way beneath our feet without warning, without pity.

"I've seen that boy," my son tells me. "I've seen that boy in my dreams."

"So have I," I tell him, picturing the boy's face: pink and radiant as he emerges through a small opening in the middle of the river. He's a tiny Houdini, amazing the world. He cries a bright cry.

"I'll look for him," my son says. "I'll pull that boy up with a rope. When I get bigger I'll find him, and bring him home."

6

In late winter, we wake in the morning and the temperature is warm, so we go for a walk again by the river. The sun makes the thinning ice glisten. Beneath the surface, the river rushes.

"What happens if I shout across the river?" our son asks. "Will it echo back?"

"I doubt it," I tell him. "But you can try."

He shouts toward the far bank. A silence.

"You and Mom try it," he says. "Your voices are louder."

So my wife and I shout his name, but the sound doesn't echo.

We walk along the shore and look out toward the water, waiting for something to come back to us.

*   *   *

"Tell me again about the boy who drowned," he asks at dinner.

"It's only a story," I say. "Don't think about it."

At that moment, I recall how my father gave me advice that day when I was too afraid to step out of the old Plymouth and onto the frozen lake. "Just don't look down when you walk," he had said. "Pretend you're on solid ground." I remember grabbing onto his hand as I eased myself out of the car.

7

That boy never drowned, I think. Each night in my dreams, the boy falls through the jagged mouth of the ice, and each night I pull him out with my bare hands. When I drag him to shore he sits up, spitting words filled with river water that I can't understand. For a moment, his face is my father's face, then it's my own face, then it's my son's, and then it's the face of some strange boy I've never seen.

"Don't you know ice from ground?" I gasp, but he stares at me blankly, not hearing.

*   *   *

Today, standing on the shore, my wife and I pause, hold tight to each other as we think about the drowned boy. For a moment, I feel like I'm standing with one foot on the shore, one foot on ice. I wish

I could explain it to our son. We call him, and he runs toward us; we each grab one of his hands and stare into his clear eyes.

He breaks free of our grasps and skips ahead, laughing. Standing at the edge of the shore, he leans toward the river and throws small pebbles onto the last sliver of ice. He never holds our hands for long when we walk near the river.

SKIP REMEMBERS

The Waking of the Carrots

■ ■ One evening before dinner, my four-year-old son opens the refrigerator and finds them: the carrots have sprouted in the vegetable bin. Just since last week, tiny white tendrils have appeared all over their thin, orange bodies.

He holds one in his little fingers and marvels at it. How did they know the long winter was over, he wants to know. How did they know that the snow is beginning to melt, and that it's the last day of March and sixty degrees outside?

We line the carrots up on the kitchen table side by side.

"We can't eat them for dinner," my son tells me. "They're trying to grow into new carrots. We have to save them," he insists, and it's impossible for me to disagree.

I stare at them and wonder how they knew to sprout—what woke them inside their sealed plastic Sno-Boy bag, inside the closed vegetable drawer, in refrigerator darkness?

*　*　*

My father cannot sleep lately. When we visit him at Easter, he tells us about it. He's retired now from his traveling sales positions and his various odd jobs. Now he putters with his woodworking and craft projects—making framed pictures—and watches TV. He explains how, at two or three every morning, he wakes and can't fall back asleep. His mind starts working, he tells us.

*　*　*

My son has an idea as we stare at the carrots. He wants to slice off their tops and see if they'll grow. So I cut a few carrots, fill the bottom half of a milk carton with potting soil from the basement, and plant the one-inch tops. He's excited as he pushes each one into the soil. "Let them see the sun," he tells me, so I balance the carton on a narrow windowsill.

"They'll grow," he says.

"I don't know," I warn.

"They'll grow," he assures me.

Mornings, he rushes down from sleeping and anxiously looks at them, and I realize he was right. Tiny yellowish-green sprouts have appeared on the dull orange tops of the carrots. As soon as we wake, we look toward the windowsill. We water them before breakfast, and my son's laughs burst in the air like bubbles. After a week, I have to remind him not to tend them so often; some days the soil overflows with a layer of water.

*　*　*

In my father's living room, I tell him how I can no longer sleep late like I used to. Now that I'm older, I wake at six or seven each morning and can't go back to sleep, though I don't have to be up until eight. I tell him I can't imagine those summer days, back in high school, when I would sleep until noon. He shifts his large frame on the La-Z-Boy. I notice his bald head has a few wisps of white on the sides. He shakes his head; he wonders, too.

Later that evening, my wife and I walk past my father's upstairs bedroom and notice he's been storing his workshop supplies in there. There's barely room to walk around the bed—it's surrounded by stacks of wooden picture frames, plaster casts of praying hands and Madonna and child, boxes of wood and glue, plastic cases of screws and bolts, bags full of nails.

* * *

The next morning, Dad says he's taking our son to the backyard for a walk. It's still chilly out, but Dad dons his green-and-black woolen coat and a green corduroy cap. He lifts his grandson to his shoulder. "Careful of your back," my mother warns. My Dad ignores the comment as he turns and steps outside. At the edges of the yard, they look at the first buds on the small trees. There's still a layer of melting snow on the ground. They stroll, pulling a few branches from a willow, then walk back with bouquets of sticks. In the kitchen, my son says Grandpa should water those trees each morning. "He's right," my father agrees, "I should."

* * *

Our son still sleeps the sleep of a baby. Lately my wife and I tiptoe in some nights and admire his face—it's so relaxed and angelic when he's pulled deep by the net of sleep. He sleeps twelve hours a night, and sometimes we have to cut off his dreams by shaking him gently. I always hate to do that, but I love to see the clean whites of his eyes when he looks up at me through his thick blond hair, then remembers, and whispers that one word. "Carrots," he says.

* * *

We return home after the Easter weekend and notice that one of the carrot tops in the plastic container has not sprouted. "Why?" my son asks. I'm not sure how to answer him.

* * *

This past week, I've been waking early in the morning, and sometimes my restless mind rushes with thoughts, and I can't fall back asleep. It's early April, and though the evening air is cool, our son

159

stays in the backyard after supper, playing in the dirt until well beyond dusk.

Two months ago, when I told my son spring would be coming soon, he asked: "What is spring?" I couldn't answer him very well then. But now, if he'd ask, I'd give him a simplistic answer, telling him it's a time when all the snow melts, a time when things think about growing again. A time for waking, for carrots.

Late at night, when I can't fall asleep, I ask myself the same question: what is spring, anyway, but a sound far inside a person that no one else hears, a sound like a humming, a longing music deep inside the roots of earth?

* * *

It's May already, and I've been thinking a lot lately about those carrots. My son doesn't need to wonder about them—he simply admires them and touches the brilliant green lacework of their leaves that uncurl day by day.

But I'm sure I'll wonder about them a long time, wonder how it must feel to be reaching out in an aluminum bin, not knowing if they're in soil or simply a strange, gray air. I'm not certain, but I think it must feel the way a blind man, waking at dawn, feels when he sits up and knows there is a morning somewhere behind all that darkness. So he listens. He listens, and moves his hand toward what calls him. Yes, it must feel something like that.

SKIP REMEMBERS

The Hunting Jacket

■ ■ The pheasant, flushed from the hollows of the high, tindery grass, fluttered straight into the barbed-wire fence and tangled itself there. At that moment, my father fired the shotgun, and a globe of smoke rose, hovered a few seconds above his head.

* * *

One week before, Dad had walked into the house with the .410 shotgun he'd bought from a man in town. Excited, I ran into the kitchen; I was eight, and I'd never seen a gun up close before. He lowered the shotgun ceremoniously onto the kitchen table and we bent over it, admiring the long, bluish-gray barrel, the whorls and knots in the varnished wooden stock.

"I haven't been hunting since I was a kid," he told me later as he polished the barrel with a soft cloth. "Can't even remember what it's like." He lifted his gaze to me. "It's time you learned, too," he said, and I nodded at him with expectation.

*   *   *

The next Saturday morning, before dawn, we drove north of town. We passed farms with slate-colored houses, pastures with horses poised still as photographs, and, behind them, the tall skeletons of windmills.

Dad had bought a green hunting jacket at the outlet store just for the occasion. As we drove, he told me it reminded him of the old army jacket he used to wear in the war.

"What happened to that jacket?" I asked. I'd seen the black-and-white World War II pictures of my dad, wearing his army jacket, leaning proudly against his jeep on the Burma Road.

"Don't know," he answered. "Guess I just lost it somewhere after the war."

When we reached the field, ten miles out of town, Dad pulled the Plymouth beneath a lone oak with overhanging branches. As though the sky had suddenly cracked, rays exploded from a pink crescent as the first edge of sun rose over the horizon of cornfields. The light slid across the oak tree, setting fire to the orange-tipped leaves. At that moment, I remember thinking that there could be no place on earth more peaceful.

Dad and I gathered the shotgun and the shells from the trunk and headed into the field. As we walked, Dad showed me the four large inside pockets of the hunting jacket, each one with a flap on top of it.

"See these?" Dad said. "These are in case you get a lot of game."

"You put the birds in your *pockets?*" I asked incredulously.

"Sure," Dad chuckled. "You could carry four pheasants in here, if you had to."

"But what about the blood?"

He didn't reply for a few seconds. "Hunters don't worry about that," he finally said.

We walked along the edge of the field, the shells in the bottom of Dad's pockets clicking together with each step. In a clearing,

162

he showed me how to aim down the barrel, hold my breath, then squeeze.

We reached a fence, and, after handing the shotgun to me, Dad eased his leg over the barbed wire. Straddling the fence, Dad suddenly ducked to one side, tearing his pants leg on the barbed wire.

"Don't ever point a gun toward anyone," Dad shouted, grabbing the shotgun. "You hear me? Not ever."

I stood there, stunned. I didn't realize I had held the shotgun with the barrel aimed at my father's chest.

As we kept walking, I couldn't get my father's expression out of my mind: his eyebrows were thin arched crescents of surprise and fear, his mouth frozen open as if he were gasping his last breath.

Half an hour later, we climbed a small grassy knoll near a fence at the far end of the field. Suddenly a pheasant burst from the grass and caught itself in the lines of barbed wire directly in front of us. The bird fluttered there a second as Dad instinctively raised the barrel and pulled the trigger. A globe of smoke rose, hovered a moment above his head. Then I heard Dad groan. His face went slack as he walked to the dead bird, still dangling from the wires. He touched it with his fingertips.

"We got it!" I cheered as I danced toward the bird. I pushed in front of dad to get a closer look.

"Damn thing never had a chance," Dad said, lowering the shotgun to the dried weeds.

"We'll eat it for supper," I said excitedly. "Right?"

Dad didn't answer; he gently untangled the bird's wings from the barbs, and with a sigh, eased it into the large breast pocket of his jacket.

A few minutes later, I asked, "How's it feel in there?"

"Still warm," he told me, breaking a layer from his face just to say the words.

We didn't see another bird the rest of the morning. Every few minutes, Dad glanced inside at the pocket of the green jacket. When I peered in at it, I could see the blood stain, spreading.

Back at the house, we cleaned the bird in the cellar. Dad laid newspapers on the dank cement floor and gutted the bird with a kitchen knife. The creases on his face deepened as he pulled out the lead buckshot with tweezers. He mumbled that he'd probably never get them all. Down stuck to the skin of his wrists like small gray puffs of smoke.

* * *

We never hunted after that. A month later, Dad sold the shotgun. He never explained to me why he put an ad in the local newspaper; in a week the shotgun was gone.

In the spring, he bought a .22, told me it was just for target practice. We'd put tin cans on posts in the woods, and I aimed down the line of the barrel the way he had taught me. Instead of shooting, Dad would stroll back to the car to drink coffee from a thermos or listen to music on the radio, and I'd keep shooting until the ammo ran out, hitting those cans until the tin was torn to feathers.

* * *

Twenty years later, after his death, I knelt in front of the casket at the funeral with my mother. The morning sun angled through the stained glass windows of the church, bathing the pews in bright reds and purples. It was so sudden, people said after the funeral.

Afterwards, I stood by the fence in our backyard for a long time, holding my breath, squeezing the wires, thinking about how, when he had the heart attack, it must have felt like a thousand shotguns going off inside his chest.

* * *

That night after Dad and I cleaned the pheasant in the cellar, Mom baked it for supper. As I ate, I glanced over to the wooden coat peg on the wall, where Dad's hunting jacket hung limply. It was a jacket he'd stop wearing and eventually misplace. But that night I could still see, on the left side, the dark, circular stain that had dried in rings.

Dad didn't talk much at the table as he chewed, except to say that the bird tasted a little strong. All through the meal, he reached into his mouth, pulled out the small gray pellets we'd missed, placed each on the side of his plate with a click.

A Road So Close to Home

SKIP REMEMBERS
One Egg at a Time

■ ■ My father's large, bony hand was not perfect. Nor were his knuckles, protruding a little more each year through his pudgy fingers. His hand was not perfect, the blurred blue veins beginning to show through the translucence of skin.

Late that Saturday morning when I was seventeen, my father stood in front of an aluminum *Mirro* pan at the old Philco stove, slowly making my breakfast. I slumped in a chair at the kitchen table in my rumpled T-shirt, yawning, waiting for him. I was beginning to get irritated with his actions, wanted him to hurry up with the breakfast so I could leave the house and meet my buddies. Steam from the coffee pot rose, and the scent swirled, faintly pungent, in my nostrils, while my father, standing in his white undershirt and brown trousers, cracked an egg against the porcelain surface of the stove.

* * *

It didn't occur to me then that the egg is a perfect shape. But it occurs to me now: an egg has its own beauty, its own inner strength; if you hold an egg lengthwise between your thumb and index finger, you'll never be able to crush it. Not even the strongest person can crack an egg while holding it by its ends; the lines of the egg are too exact and streamlined and strong.

*   *   *

When my father cracked the egg, he turned it on its side, where he knew it was weaker, its shell thinnest. Everything has its vulnerable side; he knew that, especially after years of bringing up a son, of telling me the rules he knew I might not obey. After all, I was seventeen and on the verge of a life I didn't understand. Somehow he knew I'd ignore his rules about driving too fast, chugging slippery cans of beer in the car with my buddies, staying out past my curfew. He didn't seem surprised that the football coach would catch me sneaking Kools behind the brick wall of the high school. Somehow my father knew that I'd throw stones at distant windows that were out of my range and that I'd hit them anyway.

But he never let on what he knew that late Saturday morning, my mother gone to the Laundromat, when he made me those eggs. He didn't lecture me, even though I came home two hours past curfew and slept until eleven, even though I know he was up at his usual six a.m., feeling the slow ache of a son pulling away from him. Instead, he just did what the moment called for: cracked one egg on the side of a stove and let the yolk pour carefully into the pan without breaking. It bothered me that he always had to be so methodical. But he told me once that the eggs would fry better if you made one at a time, that some things were better if you dealt with them slowly. I remember feeling impatient that morning, but mostly my head was swirling with images from the night before: the loud squeal of the rock guitars at the school dance and the smooth oval faces of girls and the metallic taste of the sweaty cans of beer behind the Woolen Mills. Then my thoughts jumped ahead to meeting my buddies downtown where we'd hang out, sipping cherry Cokes and listening to the *flick* and *bing* of the pinball machines. Someone would play a rocking Mitch Rider or Rolling Stones song on the jukebox and my shoulders would sway to the music. My head filled with every thought except what was happening at that moment: my father, leaning toward that stove, lifting the lid on the pan to check the single egg, which began to sizzle in the butter as the burner heated.

We didn't talk while he made my breakfast that morning. While the egg cooked, he glanced up at the bare plaster walls that rose to meet the high ceiling of the kitchen. Then he stood near me with the percolator of coffee, offered me some by raising it slightly in the air. I declined with a shake of my head and nodded at the milk instead. Milk: the drink of a boy. He poured me a tall glass, the white foam of bubbles bursting silently at the top of the glass, then poured himself another cup of coffee, black, carried it to the stove and glanced under the silver lid at the spattering egg, which was almost done. I remember him jerking his arm back quickly, the hot grease splattering the skin of his wrist.

I could hear the vague murmur of the old Zenith television in the den, and, through the open screen door, the barking of Mrs. Fenske's dog, chained in the yard where it had worn a circle of dirt. In the pause between those sounds I heard the call of a crow. Then I drowned out those sounds with the rock song still in my head from the night before—The Animals chanting something about getting out of this place, if it's the last thing we ever do.

One egg finished, he turned his stocky body from the stove, carried the pan toward me, tipped it, and the egg slid onto my china plate.

"How's that look?" he said.

"Okay," I said, biting off a yawn.

"Does it look okay?" he said, looking into my eyes that tried not to meet his.

"Yeah," I muttered, wondering why he always had to repeat.

And that was it. A first morning conversation, a one-sided moment of giving and taking.

I began eating that egg, and in the silence of the eating, between the murmurs of the TV, I heard the next egg break—a quick, simple sound that seemed to echo off the high plaster walls. And that sound, which might have been music, simply bugged me. *Jeeze*, I

One Egg at a Time

thought, *why does he always fry them one at a time? Can't he just hurry up for once in his life?*

My father: making the eggs one by one, tossing the shells into the brown paper grocery bag placed next to his feet. My father, taking his time, paying attention to details, probably noticing the beauty of each egg before he broke it, its shape and proportion and balance, a marvel of nature. My father, probably wondering about what might have hatched from that particular egg if it were not taken from the chicken. And then there was me: All I wanted was to stand up from the table. All I wanted was to push on an accelerator and feel the speed press me into the upholstery, to go where I wanted to go, and to get there right away.

*　　*　　*

Years later, I stood at my father's graveside in a clearing among tall pine trees. I looked at his flag-draped coffin and listened to the sound of one distant crow. I stared as they lowered the coffin into the grave with chains, and those few seconds lasted too long—I wished everything would pass and I could be in the future some-where, wished I could be anywhere but right there, right now. I realized I should have stretched out some of the other moments from years ago, not forgotten them so quickly. I should have slowed things down, savored their taste. I tried to focus on the sound of one distant crow, its incessant cawing. I tried to picture its nest, a roughly woven collection of straw and string with a few speckled eggs in it. Then the crack of the VFW rifle salute shattered my thoughts.

*　　*　　*

"Finished?" my father said, eyeing my china plate where I'd stabbed at and eaten the first egg with my fork. Not used to talking much, we said lots of things for no other reason than we thought we should say them.

"Um hmm."

Then he leaned over me, tilting the frying pan again, and the second egg, still sizzling slightly, slid onto my plate.

*　　*　　*

A Road So Close to Home

I didn't understand that those few minutes might have been as close to perfect as any moment of my youth. My father's hands weren't perfect, but that moment was. And I just sat there, my elbows denting the plastic tablecloth, anxious to get going. I simply let the moment roll past me, in its oval shape, and then it was gone.

I hunched over that second egg, my fork clicking on the plate, chugged my glass of milk, then pushed myself away from the table and stood up.

"Where you going, Skip?" he asked, his back to me as he faced the sink. He turned the faucet on and the cold water hissed as it rinsed the hot frying pan.

"Don't know. Someplace."

He turned toward me. "How was that second egg?" His broad face tried to brighten a little.

"Okay," I replied automatically, walking toward the wooden screen door. In the back of my mind, I thought I should have said more, but I didn't. And I know now that he might have wanted to say more, too. He might have wanted to put his leaden palm on my shoulder, but instead he didn't move, just faced me, paunchy in his white undershirt, arms at his sides. Nothing could stop me from going where I had to go, nothing could stop me from stepping across that small, dirt-patched yard and into my future.

I pushed hard against the screen door that morning, then paused for an instant on the front step. Inside that pause, I might have listened to the silence in the kitchen as my father stood there. Or I might have listened to the sounds outside: the barking of a chained dog, the rising and falling song of a lawn mower, the caw of some distant crow. Instead, I only heard the door crack shut behind me as I hurried toward my waiting car.

SKIP REMEMBERS

The Ones That Got Away

As my six-year-old son lifted the bass from the Mississippi into the air, the fish slapped its fin against his hands and wrists, opening and closing its mouth, trying desperately to breathe the bitter transparent ocean of air it had just been pulled into.

A few minutes before, as I knelt over the tackle box on the bank, my son asked to cast his line into the Mississippi again. I checked my watch.

"Please," he begged. "Just one more time."

My son hadn't had a bite all afternoon, just kept snagging his line in the rocks along the shallow rapids. "Okay," I said, and turned to pack up the tackle box Dad gave me years ago. I gazed at the rusty hinges, the loops of lines and leaders spilling over the edges, the loose hooks snagged in clusters in the corners.

When I heard my son shout I turned to see his fishing pole bending toward the water again.

"A fish!" he called. As he began pulling it steadily toward shore, I got a glimpse of the big bass flashing silvery and green near the surface. I grabbed the net and rushed to the edge of the river. As he reeled it closer to the shore, the fish cut broad circles in the water, swaying back and forth on his line like a pendulum.

"I can't pull it in," he said to me, his voice desperate.

I waded in up to my ankles. My wet shoes didn't matter; I couldn't let him lose that fish. The fish came in close, puffs of silt exploding beneath its tail fin in the shallows; then it seemed to spot my feet and swerve back toward the deeper water. At that moment I lunged, scooped the fish with the net to the sound of my son's cheer.

At home, my son posed for a picture in the low evening sun. He stood in front of the tree on our front lawn, pulled the exhausted three pound, fifteen-inch bass from the bucket and held it by the stringer. Then I told him to bring the fish nearer to his face and look at it, and I edged in for a close-up. My son stared deep into the fish's eye for a few seconds, and, for its last few seconds, the fish seemed to be staring back.

What each one saw, I'm not certain. Through the lens, I marveled at the multicolored markings on the bass, how beautiful the fish looked, even at the moment it was dying. I snapped the shutter.

That evening, we ate the fish for dinner. The neighbor kids stayed for the cooking ceremony while the fish, in the center of a big electric frying pan, sang its song of sputtering and popping. My son swore it was the best fish he'd ever eaten.

During the next weeks, I took a few more pictures with the camera until the roll was finished, then stepped into the dim bedroom to remove the film. I opened the back panel and gasped to see that the camera was empty—there was no film inside.

"Look," I said, holding up the empty camera. "The counter was working, but no film."

"What about that picture of my fish?"

"I'm sorry," I sighed.

When he hung his head, I put my hand on his shoulder. "You'll just have to *remember* it," I said. "You can always remember."

"No I can't," he replied, squirming away from me. "I can't remember it as good as a picture."

2

That night, I thought about the time when I was in high school and my father found his old camera in the attic and discovered it still had film inside. When we got them back from the drugstore in a paper envelope, the whole family gathered around the kitchen table as Dad held up the glossy black-and-white prints. We laughed as we saw ourselves young again: frozen somewhere decades ago, we three kids were babies, and my mother and father were thinner, the creases erased from their faces.

"Amazing they still turned out," Dad said, picking up a print of our family. "Look. The lighting's perfect on this one."

3

After I discovered the camera was empty, I set my son on my lap and tried to describe that fish. I know I cost him the memory of the first big fish he ever caught, and I wanted him to forgive my mistake. I wanted to tell him everything I could remember about that fish—the color, the markings on the face, every detail. I told him I'd write it all down for him some day.

"It was fifteen inches long," I began.

"No," he corrected me. "It wasn't that small. It was *this* long." He held his hands up, two feet of space between them.

4

Lately I've been thinking about that fish, thinking about its thin tail moving back and forth as if pushed by a slight wind. I think the bass was already dying in the galvanized pail on the drive back to the house. When my son held it, its fins were like tiny translucent wings that would never fly again. Its gills where shut tight after trying so long to pull and pull at the dry air. Its curved, primitive mouth was still clamped onto the red-and-white plastic stringer. I remember the angle of the sun and the intense blue background of the sky behind my grinning son and the fish. It was a perfect picture. The vivid colored markings on the fish scrawled across its face like hieroglyphs. Its dark, opaque eye seemed like a hole that leads to the center of the earth. A few minutes later, after the fish died, the eye turned whitish and milky. My son noticed the difference, asked me, "Why did its eye change color?"

I wasn't sure what to tell him. It was as if the fish was looking into itself. Or maybe it was seeing further than it had ever seen before: all the way to the river, through the current of the Mississippi, to the gulf, to the whole ocean.

5

The summer of sixth grade, my dad and I were fishing from a canoe in a lake when suddenly I felt a tug on my line. I reeled in a little, but the line was taut; I was certain I had snagged a log. Then, slowly, the line began to sway in the water. I worked the fish back and forth beneath the canoe for a few minutes.

"That must be *some* fish," Dad exclaimed.

I finally brought it closer to the surface near the side of the boat. "We bring a net?" I asked.

"No, I forgot it. Don't worry, we'll get him." He slid over to my side of the boat. "Easy," Dad said, coaching me. He tried to cover his excitement, but I could sense it in his voice. "Don't let the line go slack. I'll help you land it."

When the fish rose, I could see the top of its broad green back, its fin churning the water as it surfaced for an instant—the biggest walleye I'd ever seen. His mouth was huge and cavernous; his marble-like eyes glared at me. Dad lunged, trying to grab it with his hands, and in that instant, the fish whipped its head with one quick back-and-forth motion, as if it were saying no. It snapped the line, and dove into the dark green lake, disappearing.

I gasped in disbelief.

"Sorry," Dad kept saying.

I rode silently as we drove home on the county road in the Plymouth. "You're always going to lose some," he said to me. "Believe me, I know. But that was a tough one to lose. We should have had a net."

"It's okay. It's not your fault," I assured him. "That old fish line probably would have snapped anyway."

"Never should have reached for it," he muttered, shaking his head.

6

Today I make it a point to talk to my son about his Grandpa so he won't forget. I tell him all the fishing stories, about the ones we caught and the ones that snapped the line when we reached for them. The fish get bigger each time I describe them, and the stories get tangled, but he listens anyway, as if they're all true.

7

Sometimes I wonder what my son saw when he stared into the eye of that big bass.

I wish we had the photo of that fish so that, some day, when he's much older, he'll look back on it and recall every detail. Not just that he caught a fish in a river one day, but every detail: not just that its face was brightly colored, but the green and red and yellow dots on the kelly green background. Not just the long, sleek body, but the way it moved like a slice of green river water. Not just the sun, but the way it ignited every color and texture of the scene. But now the most I can do is write it down, put it on this pale white paper to help him remember, to help him see it, just a little, in his mind.

And maybe that's the most you can expect—to see the thin slices of moments clearly. Not perfectly, not wholly, but clearly. To see them in black and white, or, if you're lucky, in color; to paste those moments one by one into an album until you fill a page.

8

A week after my father's death, I noticed my camera in the closet and remembered that I'd taken a roll of photos during the previous year. I wasn't sure what pictures were inside, but I knew there'd be at least a few images of my father: they might be from last March as he peered into the new tackle box we got him for his birthday. Or from Easter Sunday when he stood stiffly in the backyard, one hand

174

on the waxed fender of the Plymouth, while, behind him, the first green buds exploded against a deep, bright azure.

As I held the camera, I thought of how, in a few days, I'd bring home the developed prints. I thought of my wife and son and I, gathering around the kitchen table, the yellow shafts of late sun angling through the parted drapes. I imagined my son, sliding the prints, one by one, from the envelope, and for a few seconds, my father would be there, alive in my son's hand again.

SKIP REMEMBERS

Seven Stories about the Old American Cars

1

It was in a dream. At least I think it was a dream, a dream of driving for hours on a smooth asphalt road in the old Plymouth. It was night, and I drove a deserted road outside Cosmos, the car skimming beneath pale layers of fog that hovered a few feet over the road. In the dream, I kept pushing on the accelerator, but it seemed as if there was always more space between the accelerator pedal and the floor.

Suddenly, the car began to slow. I had to keep pushing harder with my right foot to keep the car at the same speed. So I moved both feet to the accelerator. The next thing I knew I was slipping into the floorboard as if I had stepped into a vat of thick tar. I sank to my ankles, my knees. The car continued to slow as I sank to my hips, my chest. I clung to the wheel, but after a few seconds the pull was too much, and I let it go.

I slipped all the way under. For a moment I felt it: fear, but not just an ordinary fear. It was fear honed to an edge, fear that seemed perfected by danger and blindness and speed.

Then I felt the hands on my shoulders, pulling me up, hands I recognized by touch—my father's hands, rough and gentle, pulling me back into the driver's seat again.

I blinked at him, leaning toward me from the passenger's side, his hand steadying the steering wheel.

"Jesus," Dad scolded, "Concentrate on the road, will you? You could get us killed, you know."

Still in a daze, I nodded.

"Don't ever let go of the steering wheel again, Skip," he said. "Not ever."

2

When I was sixteen, my father claimed he could tell how fast I was driving his new Chrysler by looking at the bug smears on the windshield.

We walked out to that big luxury car that he loved and treated so well, driving it prudently, steadily, within the limits of the law. "See these streaks?" he said. "You must have been doing at least eighty or ninety. I can tell by how long they are."

If I had been speeding, I would have admitted it immediately. But, the night before when I took my buddies out to the lake, I kept the car right at the speed limit.

"I wasn't speeding," I said defensively.

"You sure about that?" He leaned toward the windshield, ran his finger along the yellow and white streaks from the insects. "These sure look like they were struck at a high rate of speed."

"I'm sure," I said, trying to sound offended. But I wasn't sure. Deep down, for some reason, I wasn't quite positive.

3

If you've ever tried it, you know what I mean. If you've ever been on a country road with a car full of guys late on a Saturday night, you'd understand. Sometimes the country roads wait in their darkness, calling you. It starts as a simple idea, a dare someone mutters. "Hey," your buddy says, "turn off the headlights." Then he says it again, and someone else agrees. "Yeah. Come on, try it. See what happens."

It doesn't seem right, but because the car is filled with your friends and you're all seventeen, squeezing cool sweaty cans of Schlitz, and because it's a hot summer night and the road is dark and empty, you finally push in the chrome button and click the lights off. For that first instant, you're driving at 80 m.p.h. in total darkness. The car is suddenly silent, and you could be anywhere—you could be in outer space; you could be driving deep under the earth, the layers of soil pressed to the windshield. Then you feel the silent panic, the not knowing which way to adjust the steering wheel. You wish for a few shivering pinholes of stars. You hope the road doesn't curve soon.

Then the silence is cut by a sound. Someone is laughing. It's your best buddy, the guy who dared you in the first place. There's nothing to do but join him, so you laugh, too, softly at first. In a moment, everyone in the car is laughing uproariously. You laugh louder, with a higher pitch, and throw your head back because, right now, it doesn't matter if you look through the windshield or not.

4

When I was in high school, I had a recurring dream:

I'm riding in the brown upholstered back seat of the Plymouth, the first car my dad owned. The car is speeding down a hill. I peer into the front seat and see that no one is driving the car. The wheel is rocking back and forth slightly. I wonder where my father is. I know I should grab that wheel, but I'm too small to climb over into the front seat, and all I can do is stare in terror through the windshield as the car rushes faster and faster down the hill.

I told the dream to my high-school counselor. "I wouldn't worry about it," he said. "A dream is just a dream. Sometimes they're just stories that don't mean anything."

5

When I came home from school one afternoon, Dad stood waiting for me in the driveway.

"You've been drinking beer in this car." He said it as though telling me a casual fact.

"What do you mean?" I said.

"Come here," he said, sauntering over to the car, where the door of the driver's side was open. He slid into the driver's seat, reached up and touched the visor. "There's beer spray on this visor," he said accusingly. "You drank beer in here, didn't you?"

I looked into the car, saw the spray marks on his aqua visor, knowing I drank that can of malt liquor in the front seat the weekend before. The can, hidden under the seat, had been jostled by a ride on a rough dirt road, and when I cracked open the pop top, the beer sprayed out.

"Yeah," I admitted, staring at the tires, "I did."

He slid out from the driver's seat. "Give me your set of keys," he said, his face growing taut, like putty hardening, as I dug for the keys from the pocket of my letter jacket. "You won't be doing any driving for a long time."

I walked for weeks during the fall of senior year. Or I bummed rides with my friends, who laughed at me for not having wheels on Friday nights.

*   *   *

Two years later, when I was cleaning the dash and windshield of the Chrysler one Sunday afternoon, I saw those spray marks on the visor. I had forgotten all about them. I reached up and dabbed at them with my damp cloth. When I pulled the cloth back, they were still there.

I lifted the Windex bottle and sprayed the marks. They didn't come off. I touched them with my fingertips. I shook my head and wanted to laugh. Those marks had *always* been there. They were imperfections in the vinyl that would never wipe away.

179

6

On the west end of Cosmos, there's a cement overpass where the train track crosses the road. "Every town has one," my father once said. Our overpass is in the middle of a curve, and the pavement narrows and squeezes through the abutments. High on the cement, near the tracks, are layers of sloppily painted words; "Class of '87" is painted atop "Class of '86" and "Class of '85." Beneath that, "'84 Forever!" is vaguely visible.

One Saturday night a car smashed into the concrete and three teenaged boys were killed instantly. I was too young to drive then, but I heard the story repeatedly from my father. He told me how they crashed into the abutment at eighty or ninety miles an hour.

When I got my learner's permit, Dad retold the story, and then ended with a warning. "They were drinking lots of beer," he'd say. "The cops found a dozen cans crushed in the front seat with the bodies."

*   *   *

Now that I'm older, I drive toward that underpass some evenings. On the side of the road, the river's current seems to be holding still in the moonlight, like something hardened and cooled. The graduating classes still boast: *Class of 2001, 2005 Rules*. I catch myself staring at the jutting concrete as I slow and coast through. I catch myself noticing the grooves and paint smears where chrome and steel once tried to push their way through thick concrete. I try not to think about it: *every town has one.*

7

After we were married, my wife and I bought a small, economy car. I'd drive to my parents' house to visit on weekends and pull my tiny Celica next to the Chrysler he kept parked on the grass of the lawn, the shiny coat of wax trying in vain to keep the paint from fading. Those afternoons, Dad still gave me tips on maintenance—wheel alignment, the best oil to use, how to measure tire tread using a Lincoln penny. He was always so confident about keeping his cars running smoothly.

*   *   *

The past few nights I've been haunted by a recurring dream. I'm driving alone in an old car on a deserted country road. The night is moonless, starless. The yellow beam of the headlights reaches ahead of the car, then, a hundred feet ahead, the light tatters.

I see a figure ahead of me on the shoulder—it looks a lot like my father, and he seems to be raising his hand. I'm not certain if he's hitchhiking, or telling me to slow down, or simply waving as I pass. When I pull over and glance in the rearview mirror, there's no one back there. *Maybe it wasn't him after all*, I think, *just a shadow from that small twisted tree on the roadside.*

I accelerate onto the road again. I grip the wheel, grip it, steady. On a straightaway, I reach forward to push the headlights off. The moment my fingers touch the button, I always wake.

My fingers never push that button, not in the dozen times I've had that dream. I wake, angry that I never get to ride with the lights out a few seconds, angry that I never get the chance to see if I can drive alone into that blackness, without laughing, and still be certain about where I'm going.

181

SKIP

Fishermen Never Have Much to Say

At dusk, when he shuffles toward the middle of the lake dragging a sled behind him, piled with his auger and his poles and a bucket, I find myself squinting at him. Each evening for the past month, I've leaned forward on my blue-and-white lawn chair, the aluminum joints creaking as I watch him stop in the middle of the lake and then drill the hole in the March ice, his silhouetted body wiry and thin, his arms circling slowly. He turns his white plastic bucket upside-down, sits on it. The thing about true ice fishermen is that they always sit on an upside down bucket; the thing about them is that they can lean for hours over that small, deep hole in the ice without moving. The ice teaches them patience. And I'm learning about it, too, as I watch him. He'd probably tell me it's not how long you wait—it's what you do while you wait. But I wouldn't know, because I've never talked to him or even seen him face to face.

2

Two months ago, in the deep freeze of January, I stood on the ice of the lake in the middle of the afternoon and heard the oddest sound. I could hear a deep guttural *glunk*, a sound like a low-pitched note from an amplifier. *Glunkglunkglunk.* The sound reverberated a few seconds, then stopped. It was like nothing I've ever heard in my life—as if the lake bottom was swallowing something, or trying to say a word.

I'm a newcomer to Lake Cosmos, having owned this small cabin only a few months, and I had no idea what caused the ice to make that sound. From what people around here say, the lake only makes sounds in the spring as it's melting, the expanding water and ice in a subtle but steady battle for space. The ice presses against itself, and sometimes you might see the two slabs of ice—ten or fifteen inches thick—raised at the point of the fissure like two small glaciers locked in a slow-motion battle. One spring, as though it were alive, the ice actually pushed itself up along the north shoreline, crushing the siding of one cabin and crawling across the dirt road.

But the day I heard the noise from the lake was the middle of a wicked cold snap, the temperatures below zero every night for a month straight. I could see, by kneeling down and peering, that the ice was at least two feet thick. So what was causing the noise? Why, every twenty seconds, did the deep, frozen lake clear its throat and mutter a word? If the ancient Ojibwe tribes had heard that, they must have imagined sacred gods at the bottom. They must have had dreams of gigantic walleyes or northerns, waging war somewhere far beneath the surface. Because there were pickups driving on the ice that day, I decided that their weight, gliding across the surface, caused the sound. But late that night, sitting on my lawn chair when all the trucks were gone, I heard the same deep grunting of the lake, as if it were calling out to me in its sleep.

3

Tonight I can't take my eyes off the lone fisherman sitting out there. All the fishing shacks and pickups are gone due to warnings about the early spring melt. I sit on my lawn chair, sipping a can of beer, and I can almost feel the legs of the chair melting slightly into the lake ice, making soft, round indentations. The more I watch him, the more restless I become. *What's he doing out there each night? What does he catch? Doesn't he ever get bored?* I wonder what makes some people want to be constantly in motion, while others are happy to just sit in one place.

*   *   *

There's no way I can judge his loneliness—or his contentment—as he sits enveloped by silence. He might be no different than a Native fisherman who, hundreds of years ago, broke through the ice and fished with primitive tools. I wonder if he's pulling up any small fish. They bite infrequently in the winter; down there in the cold water, in the pitch darkness beneath the lid of ice, the fish are reduced to the slightest of movements. There's no way I can know if the only thing he pulls up with his wood-handled pole is an empty hook, a hook that glistens in the hissing light of the lantern. And there's no way he'd know that every night I sit here, studying him for hours beneath the broad expanse of crystalline stars, some of them faint and fading, some of them so sharp they could cut your skin. He only looks down, memorizing the pockmarks and subtle cracks and suspended bubbles of the ice. I get restless and wiggle my leg nervously—I keep thinking he should *do* something, not just sit there and sit there and sit there. I get impatient, thinking how the rest of the world is going on—buying, selling, building, tearing down. I think about standing, but I don't stand, not yet. *Give him time,* I think. *Give him a little more time.*

*   *   *

If this warm spell continues, the ice will be unsafe, and in a week or two, it will melt from the shore inward, like a huge, opaque eye shrinking until the lake can see again. It'll dissolve slowly, day by day, a thin lozenge that finally disappears completely.

What will he do then, without the ice to walk out on each night? The open-water fishing season doesn't begin until mid-May, two months from now, so what will he do? I picture him sitting in a cabin somewhere in front of a woodstove, gazing at his lures. Or he might spend hours untangling one rusted lure from a stray line and see it, finally, rotate at the end of a transparent thread. Will he cook Flav-o-rite macaroni and cheese in a tin saucepan over a gas burner, then fry a small crappie he's kept for months in the freezer? I picture him plucking the bones out slowly, staring at their delicate, graceful curves. Then he might read a fishing magazine the way my father used to do; perhaps he'll spend hours memorizing the strange language of lures, pronouncing them aloud, letting them roll off the tip of his tongue like honey: Gypsi Jig, Fuzz-e-Grub, Apex Marble Eye. Pulling a wool blanket over himself, he might dream of lures spinning all night, see them glimmering above him as if he's near the bottom of a lake. Will he slowly rise toward them?

4

Tonight I sit and stare at him a long time, and then, just before midnight, I can't take it any more.

I stand from my lawn chair and take a step toward the distant glow of his lantern. I want to walk right up to him. I'm not certain if he's young or old, if he's kind or hostile, but I have to find out tonight, before he leaves. There's no other way to explain it—I have to cross the slick ice in my worn tennis shoes, shuffling my feet like some old man so I won't lose my balance. I know it's a long walk, and fishermen never have much to say, but I just have to go out there anyway. The rest of the world is going on, I know, and tonight I'm walking right toward that ice fisherman.

When I finally reach him, maybe I'll just say hello and strike up an idle conversation about what he's been catching, the name of his dog that lies at his feet—the kind of things fishermen talk about. He'll talk to me about lures, and we'll begin to speak to each other in some strange, ancient language.

"Mister Twister?" I'd ask.

"Spinnerbait," he'd answer.

"Rainbow Popeye?"

"Jig-a-Whopper Walleye Hawger," he'd reply. "Blue Fox Chewee Juice. Storm Deep Thunderstick."

I'll ask him more personal questions—things fishermen don't usually talk about—like what he's leaving behind each night when he comes to this lake. I might ask about his childhood, his wife, if he has one, his children, the last thing he thinks before he goes to sleep at night. I could ask about his fears, his doubts, the last time he gazed at his father's photo, what bores a hole in his soul. And he might reply with just a look, his thick eyebrows knitted quizzically on his broad forehead. Then I'd ask: Ever want to tell the story of your life, each day burning like a filament? Ever want to figure out what it all means before those glowing days fade? He might shake his head and reply, "Who the heck are you? I don't know you, do I?"

Or perhaps, when I finally reach him, I won't have to say hello, or even a word. I'll see a silhouette that looks a lot like me—I'll recognize myself sitting there on that upside-down plastic bucket.

And at that moment the lake, almost waking from its slumber, might make a sudden, low-pitched sound like a subterranean shift in the earth, like two distant stars colliding. Then it'll subside, and we'll just sit there, looking at each other across the hole in the ice, finally knowing the answers to all our questions.

SKIP AND DWIGHT

Stargazing

■ ■ My father was a stargazer. One night in the middle of summer when I was eight years old, he led me into the backyard to see a comet in the sky. Standing in a worn white T-shirt, he adjusted the small telescope pointed toward the west beyond the wood fence. There, above the dark silhouettes of the huge elms that lined our yard, the comet appeared like a star with a whitish tail. "Wow, I can see the smoke behind it," I said to my father as I stared through the scope.

"It's not smoke," my father replied. "That trail is from ice particles. That comet's a huge chunk of ice."

Comets and meteors always fascinated my father, and he studied them in his *Popular Science* magazines. He often told me about the famous Hailey's Comet and how it wouldn't appear again until the late 1990s. When I realized how many years it would be until the comet came again, it seemed so far away. The next morning at school, while Sister Agnes lectured the third-grade class about religion and history, I wrote in thick black letters in my notebook: *Hailey's Comet, 1998*, as if I thought I'd somehow have that thin, worn notebook as a reminder years into the future.

*   *   *

That night when we looked at the comet in the sky, I was surprised by the fact that it didn't seem to be in motion. I'd always confused comets with meteors, thought that comets rushed and sparked across the sky at thousands of miles an hour.

"Why isn't it moving across the sky?" I asked.

"It *is* moving," he assured me, "but it's barely noticeable. That comet is 30,000 miles away. When we come out here tomorrow night, it'll still be up there, but a little more to the west."

When I squinted at it without the telescope, that comet didn't look much different than the other stars.

"Did you ever realize," my father sighed as we sat on the back porch, "that some of the stars we see aren't really there?" He took a sip of his lemonade, always mixed with a little limeade so it wasn't so sweet. "Some of them burned out a million years ago."

I just gave him a puzzled look.

"We're not really *seeing* those stars," he continued. "We're just looking at their light from a million years ago that's still making its way to the earth."

Then my father told me a story. "It was 5 a.m.," he began, "and the world was dark." He was delivering newspapers one early morning when he was in grade school, and while riding his bike on the sidewalk, he looked up and saw it: the whole western sky was lit orange by meteors. "There must have been hundreds of them." He raced home as fast as he could without delivering the rest of the papers in his canvas bag. "I've never seen so many meteors, before or since," he explained. "It still gives me the shivers to talk about it. It terrified me."

I pictured the sky, shredded and torn by supernatural orange claws. It was hard for me to think of my father—who never seemed to fear anything—being scared by a meteor shower.

"What were you afraid of?" I hesitantly asked him.

He didn't reply for a few seconds, shifting his heavy frame. "I thought it was the end of the world," he finally said.

* * *

My father often sat beneath the lamp in the den and read to me from his articles about the universe. I curled up next to him on the soft lavender sofa, learning the words *nebula* and *luminous* and *light-year*, listening in wonder to science facts and theories. Some nights I fell asleep to the sound of those words, which seemed to glow inside my skull: *galaxy, supernova, Alpha Centauri.* Other nights, his deep, resonant voice read to me from articles, which, though I couldn't really understand them, were as fascinating and delightful as any childrens' books: *"Stars reach temperatures of more than 20 million degrees,"* he read, shaking his head in amazement. *"Others survive for 10,000 billion years."* I knew my father always wished that he could be a scientist or an astronomer, even though he was just a salesman, selling Whirlpool washing machines. He read to me about the Big Bang theory: *"It was a huge explosion,"* he said, *"and one of those flying particles became our planet."*

"Is all this true?" I once asked.

He slipped off his half-shell glasses and stared at me, a little disappointed. "Of course it's true."

* * *

189

One evening my father read an article about the ancient astronomers. He told me that some ancient peoples believed that meteors were holes torn in the roof of the sky. One Native American tribe believed that herds of huge deer and elk inhabited the other side of the sky, and that the meteors were their hooves, scraping through the surface as they ran. They believed that when the herd of deer and elk finally broke completely through the sky, then the end of the world would come. Others thought a shooting star represented the soul of a person who had gone to the beyond with the Great Spirit; they were convinced that the Great Spirit was pointing at the earth with his index finger, tracing a bright, sparking line on the dome of the sky.

* * *

When I was a child, I didn't understand how the universe worked. I was just a small boy in a small town in the middle of a flat, endless plain, a small boy standing with his father and staring at the unreachable mystery of the sky. I was just a small boy whose face was faintly illuminated by the glow of distant ice or fire that he didn't really understand. There was no end of the world for me: for me, the world was just beginning. For me, the world was still out there waiting, somewhere outside town, where the taut plains stretched to meet the thin line of the horizon.

* * *

One Saturday at the Cosmos County Library, amid speckled marble busts of Plato and Aristotle, I searched for books about outer space-for my school report on my future career as an astronomer. I found one called *The Big Book of Outer Space* in the children's section, brought it to a thickly varnished oak table. I marveled at the aerial photo of a half-mile-wide crater in Arizona, its roundness and symmetry like a perfect pockmark on the moon. I studied a photo of a house that had been struck by a meteor in the middle of the night while the owner, a middle-aged man, was lying in bed. The man was uninjured by the meteor, the caption beneath the photo said, and it added that no person has ever been struck and killed by a falling meteor.

I couldn't wait to tell my father what I'd read. When I did, he listened intently. "Wouldn't that be something if one struck our house?" he mused. It was as if he wished he were the man in the article, as if he wished he could have been *that close* to a falling meteor, to touch the smooth surface of its cooled molten metal with his fingertips, to sense the distance it had traveled.

* * *

Before I knew it, I was in high school, and I didn't have time to look through the telescope with my father any more. That was ancient history, and all my free time was spent hanging out with friends or going to the movies on Friday and Saturday nights. When I parked in a car beneath the stars, all I could stare at were the midnight-blue eyes of the girl in the seat across from me. My father still read his astronomy books as he reclined on the La-Z-Boy in the den, but, by the time I was eighteen, I'd just saunter past him.

"Skip, look at this," he said once, excited about an asteroid article in *The Time-Life Book of Outer Space*. The article's title was: "Huge Asteroids Drift Through Space."

I glanced briefly at the illustrations. They looked like dull chunks of rock. "Oh," I said, my voice as flat as the asphalt I'd soon be driving on.

"Ever think about that?" my father said, trying to strike up a conversation. "That one of these could collide with us?" Over the years, he'd lost his hair, and as he gained weight, his face became round, moon-shaped.

"Not really," I said, trying to brush him off. I checked the glowing dial of my new watch; there was a dance at the teen center in a half-hour.

Back in the house late that night, high on the cans of beer I drank with my buddies, I saw my dad's *Time-Life* book lying open on the TV table. There, written in heavy black letters in my father's handwriting, were the words: *Hailey's Comet, summer, 1998.*

* * *

My father never lived to see the summer when Hailey's Comet slid across the sky. A few years before it, on a spring day, he passed away. It was a day like any other day, until that telephone call. My sister's voice trembled through the hundreds of miles to the receiver in my hand. I stood there, unable to speak, staring at the black phone cord that spiraled around and around.

Sometimes I want to tell the world about my father in the clearest, most elegant way possible. Sometimes I wish I could create some myths, some great legends about my father's life and what it meant to me. But I can never quite find the right way to say it. All I have are these simple words about him, these few stories falling from my lips.

All I know is that one day he was alive, and the next day he was gone, leaving a hole in the world where he'd been.

* * *

The summer of 1998, I stood in my backyard behind the porch and watched Hailey's Comet cross the deep blackness of the sky. The comet wasn't as large as I had envisioned it when I was a kid; it was wispy and distant on the horizon, and I had to peer through binoculars to see it clearly. Still, it had a beauty all its own, its graceful, pale tail like a sheet of sheer silk trailing behind it. I watched it a long time, then walked back to the house. As I did, I got a glimpse of myself in the glass of the back door; I had become large and barrel-chested like my father, and my hairline was receding. I stood there in my worn white T-shirt and realized that I'd never become a scientist like I'd always dreamed.

Suddenly, all those years since I stood with him, staring at the sky, seemed to compress into one single moment. All the years since the beginning of time squeezed together, and I was all of earth's people: I was Neanderthal, I was Ojibwe, I was twenty-first century human, I was Skip Carrigan from the tiny town of Cosmos, Minnesota.

I turned from my reflection and lifted my head toward the sky. There were too many stars, all those broken fragments drifting aimlessly through space. At that moment, I knew what my father felt that early morning before dawn on his paper route when he was startled by the meteor shower. I understood his fear and wonder, knew exactly what he meant about the end of the world. For those few seconds, terrified and suddenly lost, I felt the weight of the whole sky on my shoulders, and I wanted to drop to my hands and knees on the grass and cry.

Then something calmed me: a thought spiraled toward me, a trail of sparks glowing behind it. I remembered my father telling me, when I was eight years old, about the stars that faded so long ago, but how their soft, glowing light was still reaching us. After all those years, their light was still reaching us.